HIGH GUN AT SURLOCK

To keep from serving jail time, Vince Templeton agrees to take on a false identity and go to Surlock, Wyoming. Once there he is to work as a teamster for Charles Huxton and try to prevent a war that is brewing between Huxton's Transport and the Yates freight outfit. However, when he falls hard for Jessie Yates, he has the impossible task of winning over a girl who hates him and everyone working for Huxton. When the showdown comes, he must not only save the woman he loves, but also outshoot a deadly gunman named Phoenix Cline...

HIGH GUN AT SURLOCK

HIGH GUN AT SURLOCK

by

Terrell L. Bowers

Dales Large Print Books
Long Preston, North Yorkshire,
BD23 4ND, England.

British Library Cataloguing in Publication Data.

Bowers, Terrell L.
    High gun at Surlock.

        A catalogue record of this book is
        available from the British Library

        ISBN   978-1-84262-507-1 pbk

First published in Great Britain in 2006 by Robert Hale Ltd.

Published in Large Print 2007 by arrangement with
Robert Hale Limited

Dales Large Print is an imprint of Library Magna Books Ltd.

Printed and bound in Great Britain by
T.J. (International) Ltd., Cornwall, PL28 8RW

CHAPTER ONE

Vince Templeton had known Judge Tate for many years. The judge and his father had been close friends. Vince had struck out on his own a few years previously and had returned to Cheyenne for his father's funeral. He'd been back in town less than a week and had already managed to get himself in trouble with the law. Other than shaking hands with Tate at the funeral service, this was the first time he had faced the judge.

Judge Tate was a man of impressive size and stature. Even behind his desk and pushing fifty years of age, he appeared a formidable man. He looked over his spectacles at Vince, sighed mightily and gave a shake of his gray head.

'Vincent, I'm told you started a fight with the mayor's son yesterday.'

'Reckon that's the truth of it, Your Honor,' Vince admitted.

'What justification do you offer for engaging in a brawl with Mr Elder?'

'Your Honor,' Vince explained, 'Seth Elder

was stomping all over some young gent about half his size. I offered to give him a more fair match.'

'You offered?'

'Busted him in the nose,' he said. 'Coaxed a fight out of him right quick.'

'And then you whipped him.' It was a statement.

'Yes, sir, Judge,' Vince declared. 'Did a right thorough job too.'

Tate allowed a grim smile at his honesty and looked down at Vince's hands.

'I don't see any cuts or scrapes on your knuckles.'

'No, sir, I put on my cowhides before I laid in to him. I didn't aim to bust a knuckle on his teeth.'

'Suffice to say, the mayor is not keen about someone pummeling his boy.'

'Maybe not, Judge, but I was preventing a beating.'

'Uh-huh,' said Tate. 'You stopped a beating by dealing out a beating yourself. The combatants change, but the result is the same.'

'That's a rather narrow way of looking at it,' Vince argued. 'If a bully gets himself a whupping, it ought to be a good thing.'

Tate took a long moment, as if collecting his thoughts.

'The mayor insists I sentence you to serve time in jail.'

'If he had offered to throw me a party I'd have been a whole lot more surprised.'

'He might agree to a necktie party,' Judge Tate quipped.

Vince grinned. 'Given a choice, I'd rather do the time, Your Honor.'

'There might be another option,' Tate said. 'I received a letter in my mail yesterday, a request for help. You might be the right man for the job.'

'A job? For me?'

'I spoke to the US marshal about it, but he doesn't have a capable man to send. When I mentioned you, he agreed to let you undertake the chore.'

Vince grew wary. 'This can't be something good, else you wouldn't be holding a jail sentence over my head before bringing it up.'

'Your dad told me you worked for a traveling carnival some time back. That where you learned to fight?'

'Yep. Did some sparring with the boxing champ we had traveling with the show. I filled in for him whenever he was feeling poorly. Mostly, I stuck with trick-shooting and showing off as a fast-draw artist.'

'Your pa claimed you were the best "honest" trick-shooter he ever saw,' the judge continued to speak of his past.

'I never did resort to using special buck-shot loads to hit what I aimed at,' Vince responded. 'I don't care for cheaters.'

'He said your favorite trick was to have two people drop beer-mugs at the same time. You would draw and shoot both mugs before they hit the ground.'

'I've had to do the trick more than once somedays to get both mugs.'

Tate smiled again at Vince's honesty.

'The job is over in Surlock, up near the Wyoming border. Two freight outfits are in a battle for control of the shipping business. With a lot of gold being hauled out of the Dakotas, there is a demand for moving freight, supplies and ore. Plus, there is also a stage line. However, there isn't enough business for two different express companies. The Yates Freight Company has been working that neck of the woods for years, but H & B Transport has moved in with more men and money. There's been a killing, several robberies and wagons have been burned or wrecked. It sounds like the start of a bloody war.'

'What do you want from me?'

'The US marshal needs to appoint a deputy to look into the trouble there. This rivalry needs to be settled without any more people getting killed.'

'You want me?' Vince gasped in shock. 'To be a deputy?'

'That's the job, Vincent.'

'I'm no lawman and I've never been to Surlock, Judge. How am I supposed to go about finding out who is behind the trouble and sabotage?'

'The marshal told me Charles Huxton has hired a new hardcase to come to work for him as a teamster. He's never met Kyler Dane and I remember you hauled freight for a living a few years back. This Dane fits your description, but he won't be able to make the trip.' With a grin he added: 'The marshal has him behind bars awaiting trial in Denver.'

'So you want me to pretend to be this Dane character,' said Vince.

'That's right. Kyler Dane has his name on a wanted poster from Colorado – assault and robbery. You need to remember you robbed a saloon over at Canyon City and that you pistol-whipped the bartender.'

'Why would Huxton hire a wanted man, one he has never met?'

'I suspect he wanted a man who was good with a gun and who would do what he was told without conscience or question. Dane told the marshal he had been hired sight unseen, through a third party. He gave up the information in hopes that a judge would take in to account that he is being co-operative. He claims he doesn't know anyone over in Surlock. You only need to convince Huxton that you're desperate for a job and have a shady past. He won't doubt you're the man he sent for.'

'If I do get the job, then what?'

'Find out whatever you can. If there's crooked dealings going on, get us the proof and send me a wire. The marshal will come down and make the necessary arrests.'

Vince was still perplexed. He had gone from being a likely inmate at a jail one minute to a deputy US marshal the next. It was a bizarre adjustment. Even as he frowned in thought, Tate handed him a piece of paper and a badge.

'This pay voucher is good for a hundred dollars at any bank or Wells Fargo office,' he told Vince. 'It should be plenty to set you up, until you start drawing wages. If you find proof of criminal activity you'll have to testify in court. After that you can turn in

12

your badge and go on with your life. How does that sound?'

'Sounds to me like you ought to be the one locked up, Judge. I'm fixing to think your clock stopped at thirteen!'

Tate gave a dismissive wave of his hand.

'We don't have enough lawmen to look into every complaint or request that finds its way to our desks. The territory is too big and there simply isn't the manpower to do the job. The marshal's office hires special deputies all the time. Some are permanent, while others are employed for individual cases. This is a chance for you to do something worthwhile with your life.'

'That's it then?' Vince clarified. 'I'm to snoop around and see who is doing what. If laws are being broke, I dig up evidence on the guilty party and send word to you.'

'You've got the idea,' Tate said. Then he put a level gaze on Vince. 'What do you say, son? Are you willing to do this little job for me, or should I throw you in jail for assault and look elsewhere?'

'I don't know beans about being an undercover lawman, but it sure beats sitting behind bars for the next few weeks. I'll ride over to Surlock and see if I can convince Huxton that I'm Kyler Dane. If he takes the bait, I'll see what I can find out.'

Tate stuck out his hand. 'I know you'll do a good job, my boy.'

Charles Huxton stood at the window of the bank and stared after the two freight wagons pulling out of town. There was a good business here, but only if he eliminated the competition. He had talked big and assured his sister-in-law, Alma Bailey Huxton, that he would make her a lot of money. She expected results and was not the sort to be patient.

'What do you think?' George, the bank-owner asked, breaking into his thoughts. 'You haven't gotten many contracts from the big mine-owners to this point. Most of them are staying with the Yates family.'

'That is not your concern,' Huxton told him. 'We have a deal. I'll handle my end of things and you handle your own. I'll figure a way to get the contracts I need.'

'I didn't count on any violence,' the banker whined. 'I was fifty feet away when your man, Strap, shot and killed Cory Yates out in the street!' The man shook his head. 'That kind of thing doesn't look good, Charles. It might bring the law down on us.'

'The law can't prevent two men from having an argument, George. Besides, one less

14

Yates makes it harder for them to keep their schedules. Each time they can't make their deliveries, it affords me the opportunity to pick up another of their contracts. I didn't give Strap the order to kill Cory, but it works to our advantage.'

George was not satisfied. 'Maybe so, but I've done business with Big Mike's family ever since I opened the bank. I hate to see their family being ruined and killed.'

'It's like I told you at the beginning,' Huxton explained, 'there's room for both freight companies. I only want a fair share of the business. I need a few more contracts to haul ore from the mines and transport supplies for the numerous businessmen of Surlock. With the added business and my own stage run, I can make a go of it.'

'You still have to take the business away from Big Mike.'

'He and his family have had the run of the place since this land was settled. It's time they learned to share the wealth.'

'Yeah, I see what...' The banker ceased speaking at the knock on the office door. It opened half-way and Huxton's clerk stuck her head into the room.

'Sorry to interrupt, Mr Huxton, but there is a gentleman to see you. He said his name

15

is Kyler Dane and that you were expecting him.'

'Yes, Wanda,' he replied to the woman. 'Send him in.'

At the banker's curious frown, Huxton escorted him to the door.

'I'll talk to you later, George. This is some-one I have to speak to in private.'

'Certainly, I understand.'

Vince's heart pounded in his chest like a stampeding steer. He reminded himself, *my name is Kyler Dane. I'm a wanted man. Kyler Dane, desperado, bad guy, on the run.*

'Sir,' the woman's words jolted through him like a lightning strike, 'Mr Huxton says you can go right in.'

Kyler smothered the instant foreboding, uttered a polite 'thanks' and went through the door into a large office. A man was standing next to an imposing, burnished oak desk. Charles Huxton was a couple inches shorter than Kyler's five-ten, had a slight paunch and had thick, dark hair, except for a hint of gray above his ears. Maybe thirty or so, he was probably considered handsome or distinguished by some. He wore an expens-ive vest and suit, with shoes polished to such a degree a fellow could have used them for mirrors to shave by. His hands were locked behind his back, as if poised to make an assessment of the new arrival.

Reminding himself that he had a price on his head, Kyler paused at the entrance and took a nervous look around.

'You Huxton?' he asked.

'Come in, Mr Dane,' the man offered. 'I've been expecting you.'

Kyler said: 'I was told you needed a teamster and paid top dollar.'

'For the right kind of man, yes.'

Kyler cast an anxious glance over his shoulder and quickly closed the door.

'I pulled a chair to this game, with no cards showing on the table,' he said tersely. 'Maybe you should give me an idea of what this job is all about.'

The man reached out to a box of cigars on his desk top and opened the lid.

'Smoke?' he asked.

'I never acquired the taste,' Kyler replied.

Huxton gave a nod and studied him while he cut the tip off of the cigar. He put a match to the smoke and took a long pull before speaking again.

'You've had a little trouble in your past,' he began, 'but I'm told you're capable in a fight.'

'I've been in my share of fixes and scrapes,' Kyler answered carefully.

Huxton blew a cloud of smoke. 'Ever kill anyone?' he asked.

The bluntness caused Kyler to swallow hard.

'I'm no back-shooter, if that's what you're looking for.'

'Not at all,' Huxton responded easily. 'I am merely interested in your overall qualifications.'

Kyler shrugged. 'I reckon there are reasons for hurrying the demise of a select citizen on occasion. As for my qualifications – when driving a rig, no one is going to take anything away from me.'

'We are in competition with the Yates Freight Company. They have suffered a few mishaps and think I'm responsible. They are liable to try and disrupt our own deliveries. Hence, I need a man I can count on to get our shipments through.'

The speed of his draw was a blur. Before Huxton could blink, Kyler's gun was in his fist, the muzzle pointed at the man's chest. He smiled inwardly at the sag in Huxton's jowls and the widening of his eyes.

'Like I said,' he spoke firmly, 'no one is going to take anything away from me.'

'Hellfire, man!' Huxton exclaimed. 'I never saw you reach for your gun!'

Kyler ignored the praise, spun the gun adroitly and used a practiced twist to slip the weapon back into its holster.

'What about the pay?' he asked. 'I was promised a good wage for my services.'

'Yes, yes!' Huxton did not hide his eagerness. 'Fifty dollars a week ... plus a sizable bonus when I've collected the needed contracts.'

Kyler licked his lips. It would look as if he was thrilled at the prospect of earning such high wages, but it was actually to combat a dread anticipation. So much money for merely driving a rig? What kind of nightmare had Tate gotten him into?

'The money sounds good, Mr Huxton. You assign me a wagonload of freight and I'll sure enough get it through for you.'

Huxton stuck out his hand.

'I believe you're just the man I'm looking for, Dane. Welcome to the company.'

CHAPTER TWO

Kyler spent the next day checking over the lay of the land. His horse needed a rest, so he rented a stable nag. He returned to find the elderly hostler mending a harness.

'I was beginning to wonder if you got lost,' the man said. 'Old Nelly ain't been out for a ride in a month of Sundays. I expect she's about done in.'

'Never gave me a hint of trouble, old-timer.'

'It ain't *old-timer*, sonny,' he corrected gruffly. 'Name's Nathaniel Ethan Osborn. Folks call me Nat to save time.'

Kyler grinned. 'Well, I'm not a *sonny* either, Nat. I'm Kyler Dane.'

Nat clucked his tongue. 'Fair enough. Glad to meet you, Dane.'

'Likewise,' Kyler replied.

'I used to shag freight for a living,' Nat explained, 'but my bones can't take the jarring of a wagon any more. I opened up this livery and earn a sizable portion of my living by tending to Huxton's animals and wagons.

One of the straps was about worn through on this here harness, so I'm replacing it with a new one.'

'I'm supposed to start hauling for Huxton in the next day or two.'

'I overheard a couple of the boys talking. They said Huxton had hired a gunman who would get their wagons through, no matter what.'

'I'm no slouch with a gun, but I'm no gunman.'

'That ain't what the Wanted poster says.'

Kyler could not hide his surprise. 'Wanted poster?'

'I keep my eyes open and stay abreast of what's going on most of the time. The hand-bill was from Colorado, wasn't it.'

Rather than deny the charge, Kyler shrugged.

'I made a mistake.'

The old boy stared him straight in the eye.

'You don't strike me as the sort with a short temper.'

'No, I'm about as peaceful as a lamb.'

Nat chuckled. 'Guess even a lamb kicks up his heels from time to time, huh?'

Kyle joined in with a laugh. 'Yeah, on occasion.'

'I'm about done here, sonny. I'll let you

treat me to a beer or two and we'll be square for you borrowing Nelly for the day.'

'Sounds fair.'

'I'll also fill you in on some of the happenings here in Surlock. Wouldn't hurt for you to know the players at the table before you go betting on your hole card.'

Those words struck a sensible chord. Tate hadn't given him much information. Kyler needed someone who could tell him about the situation in Surlock. He'd buy the old gent a couple drinks and see what he could learn about the freighting war.

Strap Adere sauntered over to where Phoenix was eating his supper. Without an invite, he pulled out a chair and sat down across from him.

'You meet the new man on the payroll?' he asked.

Phoenix glanced at him.

'Huxton mentioned a new hire, but I haven't crossed paths with him as yet.'

'Boss says he's a bad man with a gun.' Strap snorted his disdain. 'What for do we need another gun? You and I can handle the Yates bunch without breaking a sweat.'

'Someone has to shag freight and see the work gets done,' Phoenix replied. 'It's sure not going to be me. Do you want to start playing teamster?'

'That ain't my point,' Strap said. 'I'm asking why we need a gun hand for the job. I took out Cory Yates slick as can be.' He puffed up his chest. 'Nailed him square in the brisket – twice – before he could even clear leather.'

Phoenix grunted his indifference. 'Cory was a kid and a freighter to boot, Strap. I wouldn't crow too much about taking someone like him in a gunfight.'

Strap scowled across the table. 'I gave him an even chance and took him clean!'

'Sure, Strap.' Phoenix almost yawned the words. 'But I'll save my praise for when you take on a real man with a gun.'

Strap hated the way Phoenix continually put him down. He was good with a gun, real good. He'd braced Yates at a mere fifteen feet. That took guts. If Yates had managed to get off even a single shot, he could have killed Strap from such a close distance. Phoenix sure ought to give him credit for his courage and speed with a gun.

'You're the big man,' Strap growled his disappointment. 'I know you was hired to scare off any opposition, but it don't mean the rest of us are a bunch of culls. I'm near as good as you.'

A hint of frost entered Phoenix's eyes.

'Anytime you want to replace me on the payroll, all you have to do is come calling, Strap. I'll give you first go.'

Strap's pride smarted, but he was no fool.

'Maybe I will one day.' He tried to put conviction into his voice, but the words came out weak and impotent.

'Don't let anything but fear of death stop you, Strap,' Phoenix suggested smoothly. 'And be sure to write a note of goodbye for your family first.'

Strap rose to his feet. He wished he had a smart comeback, but he wasn't going to push for a fight. Both of them knew who was the better man with a gun. In fact, no one was up to taking on Phoenix Cline ... nary a man alive.

Jessie Yates was clearing the table when Kenny entered the house. She had given up on any of her three brothers arriving home in time for supper.

'Jeff's on the stage route,' he said, looking around, 'but where's Mike?'

'He took the Powder Mountain run. He won't be back until tomorrow night.'

Ken pulled a chair around and sat down

heavily. 'You didn't wait for me.'

'You know I prepare supper for six o'clock. It's half-past already.'

'Sorry,' he grumbled. 'I was busy in town … checking out the latest gossip. Huxton has gone and hired himself another gun.'

Jessie groaned. 'We can't compete with the troop of gunhawks on his payroll now. What does he need with another man?'

'Supposed to be a teamster. I saw him at the saloon – he and old Nat were having a beer together. The guy looked capable. I'd say he was hired to make certain Huxton doesn't lose any of his freight.'

Jessie placed the kettle of stew on the stove to warm, then rested her hands on her hips.

'Huxton must be worried we will retaliate for our losses.'

'I'd wager you're right,' Ken agreed. 'There's no doubt he and his boys are behind our recent problems.'

'What's going to happen to us, Ken?' Jessie asked bitterly. 'We've spent every cent we have to pay for the freight that's been stolen or destroyed. We can't afford to make needed repairs on our wagons, let alone hire any more help. Now Mr Glenn, at the bank, has told Mike he can't give us any more credit.'

'Yeah, once Huxton moved in, we became a poor risk.'

'Dad would come right up out of the grave if he knew we were about to lose everything he worked for all his life.'

'It ain't right!' Ken declared. 'We were here first. We were taking care of every account in the valley and growing bigger and more secure every year. Along comes another express company and we're in a struggle to even survive. Huxton, the greedy, bloodsucking skunk, is out to ruin us.'

Jessie decided the stew was warm enough and dished up a plate for her brother. He stuck a fork into a piece of meat and stared at it.

'This is us, Jess,' he said. 'We're a plate of stew for Huxton and his gunnies to eat alive.'

'We can't give up, Ken.'

'Not until we've been chewed completely and devoured,' he added.

'We have to keep the business going,' Jessie said. 'If we can hold on to the bulk of our accounts, we can weather this through and maybe Huxton will give up.'

'If Huxton was ready to fold, Jess, he wouldn't have brought in another hardcase to bulk up his stance. The man won't be happy until we're broke and out of business.'

Jessie didn't say so, but she had to agree with Ken. Charles Huxton wanted all of the business. It was likely to be a fight to the death and, from the way the deck was stacked, her family's company would be the one doing the dying.

Just like Cory, she remembered. Tears burned at the back of her eyes, but she refused to give in to sorrow. They had always been a hard-working family. When their mother had died of fever she had taken over the chores of the household. When their father was laid to rest Big Mike had become the manager and head of the company. Nothing had deterred the Yates family from continuing the family business. Nothing, that is, until Huxton arrived.

Jessie suffered a jaded and wrung-out sensation. Everything seemed so hopeless. She fought the frailty, knowing she had to be strong for her brothers. Mike, Jeff and Ken needed her. In spite of her being the only girl in the family, she had always pulled her own weight. She frequently drove the stage or hauled shipments with the small freight wagons. At home, she kept the house running smoothly and prepared most of the meals. She had always done more than any of the boys ... except for Mike.

For a moment she wished she could relax and be a normal girl. She had spent most of her childhood competing with her brothers. Whether in roughhouse games or working in the fields, she never let them get the better of her. However, being strong and independent had its drawbacks. As she was growing up most of the guys around had shunned Jessica Yates. She had a quick temper; if she got into a situation she couldn't handle one of her brothers was right there to take care of it for her. As a result of her brothers' protective natures, the local boys were a little on the shy side about trying to court her.

At a party or one of the monthly barn dances, she had usually ended up alone. It had changed over the past couple years, as she was older and men weren't as easily intimidated as the younger boys. Plus, there was an undeniable shortage of eligible girls in that part of the country. Even so, the suitors knew she was a woman to be reckoned with. Hold her too close during a dance and Big Mike or one of her other brothers might take exception.

For a moment, she allowed her mind to linger on the notion of romance. She yearned to have a gentleman or two come calling. She would have enjoyed being able to don a frilly dress, fix her hair like a proper lady, maybe use a little rouge to bring a blush to her face. She would enjoy feeling pretty, rather than being covered in dust and smelling like a team of sweaty horses. Being forced to help with the business end of things, she seldom looked much like a lady. Nor did her riding-outfit or work-clothes present her in the most favorable light. Hence the reason she sat alone evenings and at the Sunday meetings. She was still a tomboy, the Yates wildcat.

And who wants to tame a wildcat? she wondered.

Ken pushed aside the empty plate. 'Guess I'll try and get some shut-eye. I've got to be up early, so I can relieve Jeff for the stage-run tomorrow.'

'Another of our worries,' she said. 'Huxton has ordered a new Concord coach. Once it arrives he's bound to steal many of our customers.'

'Another nail in our casket,' Kenny replied. 'His new stage might even be the final nail needed to bury us.'

Jessie cleared away his plate. 'We work day and night and don't gain a thing.'

'Yeah, we really need to hire us another driver.'

'Who is going to dare risk riling Huxton or Phoenix?'

'No one I've ever met,' Ken replied with a grunt. 'If I wasn't a part of this family, I'd have skedaddled a long time ago myself.'

'Good night, Ken.'

'Yeah, see you in the morning.'

Jessie waited until he'd left the room. Then she glanced up at the roof, attempting to penetrate through to the heavens above.

'Dear Lord,' she murmured, 'we could sure use some help. We can't win this fight alone. Don't let us lose everything our family has worked so long and hard for ... please.'

Kyler made several runs without incident, then was given time off for the town's Fourth of July celebration. Almost everything shut down operations for the special activities. It was a day for fun, music, games and eating.

Kyler enjoyed spending time with Nat Osborn. He was a cheerful sort and they took in the sights of the festival together. They happened along the main road through town when Kyler spied a striking girl on the opposite side of the street. She seemed preoccupied in deep thought and didn't notice him staring in her direction.

The young lady was attired in a dark

riding-skirt and matching short jacket. She also wore cowgirl boots and a ladies' Western-style hat. Her long, silken, auburn locks were not to be confined beneath the headgear, spilling out in a loose, flowing mane. She paused to brush at an untamed strand of hair that had blown into her angelic face and caught at the corner of her mouth.

She passed by, a mere twenty feet away, but did not look his way. Tyler whistled under his breath. There was a girl he had to meet.

'Who is that little beauty?' he asked Nat, tipping his head toward the girl.

'Dang! sonny! You're about as simple as a thimble!' the old boy jeered at his shoulder. 'You don't want to go getting no ideas about her.'

'Why not?'

'She's the one gal in the country who is sure to hate your guts.' At Kyler's confused frown, Nat explained: 'That there is Jessie Yates of the Yates Freight Company. You're working against her and her family.'

Kyler groaned. 'I begin to see I'm on the wrong side of this here fracas.'

'You're a Huxton employee, sonny boy,' Nat stated tersely. 'Your boss is directly responsible for one of her brother's being killed and is trying to ruin her whole family's business. She ain't packing nothing but a pocketful of contempt for anyone with the Huxton brand. Besides which, if'n she didn't haul off and knock you silly for making eyes at her, one of her brothers would sure enough do it. And taking on Big Mike would be about as tough as wresting a spool of barbed wire. Ain't no way you're ever going to make hay with Jessie – not in this lifetime or the next!'

Kyler ignored the warning. 'She's dressed like she is going to do some hard riding.'

'Jessie enters 'most every contest in town – the foot race, the baseball toss, tug-of-war and a few other games with the local women. I recall she won several prizes last year. She grew up playing and competing with her four brothers, so she's as good as most men at physical sports and games.'

'What about the riding-clothes?'

'She's won the horse race each of the past three years too.'

Kyler displayed a shrewd grin. 'The horse-race – it's what, a mile run?' At Nat's affirmative head-bob, he continued: 'My mare is no ordinary mount. I traded for her, back when I worked for a carnival. I've ridden her in a good many races and have never lost. In a short distance, I'm betting she's the fastest horse around these parts.'

Nat raised his brows. 'Now hold on, sonny. You ain't thinking of trying to win the gal over by besting her in a race?'

'You said it yourself: she will only see me as her enemy while I'm working for Huxton. I need to prove I'm a better man than most to earn her respect.'

Nat laughed out loud. 'Respect? For a Huxton employee?'

'It's worth a shot. She would probably laugh in my face if I went waltzing over with flowers and candy. You said she grew up with four tough brothers, so no weak-kneed milksop is going to pass her inspection.'

'You do remember way back to about ten seconds ago, when I told you one of her brothers was killed last month by a Huxton man?' Nat shook his gray head. 'Shucks, son, all that gal will see when she looks at you is someone to despise.'

'I may work for the other side, but I aim to make peace with the Yates family.'

'Kyler, my boy, for a smart young fella you ain't got the brains of a wilted daisy.'

'You wait and see, Nat,' Kyler vowed. 'I saw a poster about a monthly dance that's coming up pretty soon. With a little luck I'll have Jessie on my arm.'

'Yeah, and if your luck goes south you'll have both arms tied behind your back while her brothers hang you from the nearest tall tree!'

'I've got to give it a try.'

Nat uttered a sigh. 'Well, it's been nice knowing you, son. I reckon I won't get no fonder of you. That way, when they plant your sorry carcass in the bone yard, I won't feel obliged to mourn over your grave.'

Kyler had confidence in Nipper. She was of mixed breed with a strain of Arabian blood, blessed with both speed and endurance. She was well-rested and he had given her a double ration of oats the past evening and again during his morning visit.

When the call was made for the contestants for the horse-race, Kyler had his mare saddled, then joined the others. Nipper didn't stand out as the biggest horse, nor the best looking one in the bunch, but she was sleek and built for speed. However, she had that intangible, a burning competitive spirit. Nipper was not the sort to walk idly alongside another horse. She always had to be a step ahead, have her nose in front. It was the same whenever she ran. Once she took the lead, she kept it. Even better horses faded beside her, because she possessed the intense desire to win, always to be first.

Kyler took special notice of where Jessie lined up and smiled to himself. The gal was just like Nipper, filled with a desire to prove herself the best. Rather than attempt to draw the girl's attention, Kyler picked the end of the line for his starting position. The logic behind his thinking was on account of the single turn one half mile down the road. It would be to the inside, so he would start Nipper to the closest possible point for that turn.

Jessie was the only woman in the group of nine contestants. Poised to start the race, Kyler held a tight rein on Nipper and perceived the girl glowering his direction. She had obviously learned that he was a Huxton man. However, it was less him and more his horse that had her undivided attention. She was probably familiar with the other animals from past races. He and his mount were newcomers, so she had no idea whether Nipper was a threat or not.

'Hang on to your locks, ma'am,' Kyler said to himself, while careful not to look her way. 'You and your noble steed are in for a real challenge.'

'The race is down the road to the pole with the yellow ribbon!' the starter of the race shouted, holding his gun in the air. 'Make your turn around the pole and get back here first to win the ten-dollar purse!'

'Might as well give the money to Jessie,' a nearby rider complained. 'No one ever beats her stallion.'

'Everyone ready?' the announcer called. There was a moment's pause, then the starting-pistol was fired into the air.

Nipper was not gun-shy. She bolted forth with the others, breaking into a full run within three strides. Her unusually quick start put her immediately toward the front of the pack. Kyler was on his toes, leaning low over the saddle, his head only inches above her neck. They streaked ahead, pulling away from the others – except for Jessie. Her stallion stayed right with him.

The distance to the pole was roughly a half-mile, but it came into view after only a few seconds. Nipper felt the presence of another horse and increased her stride. Her competitive spirit soared and she stretched out to pull ahead of Jessie and her mount. The rest of those in the race were already lost in their dust.

Jessie shouted encouragement at her horse

and used her quirt, but Nipper refused to relinquish her lead. The marked pole drew closer and Kyler prepared to shift his weight. Nipper sensed something coming, but maintained her full-out run. When the pole was a hundred feet away, Kyler pulled snuggly on the reins and shifted his weight in the saddle. Nipper responded immediately, digging in with all four feet, leaning in to the turn and cutting sharply around the post. Kyler was elated with the efficiency of the maneuver, until he saw Jessie – ahead of him!

'What the...?' He was stunned until reality sank in. Jessie had made her turn before she reached the pole!

'Get her!' Kyler snarled at Nipper.

His horse didn't need motivation. The mare knew a cheat when she saw one too. They passed the remainder of the horses, still going the other way. Nipper caught her second wind and bore down on the horse ahead, eating up the ground with long, purposeful strides. She grunted from the intense effort to overtake the stallion, but the finish line loomed up ahead. They were too far behind. Nipper didn't give up, gamely pounding after the stallion, trying to close the distance. Then, suddenly, not fifty yards from the contest ribbon, Jessie pulled back on the reins!

Kyler and his horse shot past her. He jerked his head around in puzzlement as Nipper crossed the finish line a full length in front of Jessie.

There was a round of cheers from the watching crowd, all of whom were unaware that Jessie had slowed her horse at the last moment. The other riders came thundering into town behind the two of them and the race was over.

CHAPTER THREE

After accepting the winner's purse and a first-place ribbon, Kyler took his horse back to the livery. Jessie was there already, busy rubbing down her stallion. Instead of attempting to speak to her, he began to pamper Nipper. He softly praised her efforts, while using a currycomb to brush the dust and sweat from her coat and mane.

After a full five minutes of silence Jessie moved over to confront him. 'You've a very fast horse,' was her opening. 'I suppose it's necessary for a wandering gunman,' her tone grew cold, 'in case the law shows up.'

'I'm not wandering at the moment,' he replied in a nonchalant tone of voice. 'As for my mare, I've never found any quicker on a run of a mile or less.'

'What's her name?'

He glanced at her and immediately felt a weakness in his knees. The beguiling charm he had surmised from a distance had not done her justice. She was notably more attractive close up.

'Nipper,' he replied, adequately concealing his infatuation.

Her slender eyebrows drew slightly together.

'Nipper?'

Kyler displayed an impish smile.

'You don't want to turn your back or bend over in front of her. She has a mischievous way of getting your attention.'

Understanding flooded her attractive features. Jessie almost smiled, but the notion vanished at once. She rotated about and started to walk away. Kyler spoke up to stop her.

'You could have won the race,' he ventured carefully. 'If you hadn't pulled in your horse, we wouldn't have caught you before the finish line.'

She wheeled about to face him.

'I wanted to beat you,' she admitted candidly, 'but not if I had to cheat to do it. I couldn't force myself to stoop as low as you or the other stinking Huxton killers!'

'I hired on as a teamster, Miss Yates, nothing more.'

Fire leapt into her eyes. 'You were hired to break our backs and steal our family business. We were here first.'

'I'm not—'

She cut him off, hissing her words vehemently.

'We were here before there was even a town. Our express office was one of the first wooden buildings in Surlock. Everything else was wagons or tents! My uncle and his son were both killed during the Indian wars. We paid a high price for the right to haul freight and run our stage-line!'

Kyler held up his hands, palms outward, trying to fend off her verbal assault.

'Like I said, I was only hired to drive a team, ma'am.'

'Of course, I couldn't expect you to understand, not a low-life, hired gun, scavenger! It was silly of me even to think of explaining anything to you!' And with that outburst she whirled about on her heels and strode smartly out of the stable.

Kyler didn't try to stop her. He knew winning her over was going to be like breaking through a slab of thick ice. A man didn't manage it in one blow, he had to chip away a little at a time until he penetrated all the way through the dense crust.

'What do you think of the new man?' Huxton asked Phoenix.

'He owns a fast horse. I didn't think there

was an animal in the territory that could beat Jessie's stallion.'

'Speaking of the Yates family, I don't want any of our men pushing them around or causing any trouble during the celebration. This is a festive time. We don't want to do anything that might hurt our reputation around town.'

'I'll see to it,' Phoenix replied, 'but being a latecomer in the freighting business, it already makes you the usurper.'

'It's a natural response,' Huxton admitted. 'The Yates family has been around since the town was only a sprout.'

'Staying in business is going to be an uphill ride for them,' Phoenix observed. 'You've money, men and new equipment. They have worn-out rigs, a couple of their hired men have quit, and they're having a hard time handling the accounts that have remained faithful to them.'

'You sound almost sympathetic.'

Phoenix shrugged. 'I don't have any compunction about my job, but neither am I fond of setting out to ruin someone's livelihood. The Yates clan seem like decent folks.'

'I made them a reasonable offer for their business. They refused to sell.'

'Not everything is for sale, Huxton.'

'Everything and everyone has their price,' he maintained. 'Big Mike is still running the show, but he can't hold out for much longer.'

'Especially if the Yates line keeps having a run of trouble with their wagons and drivers,' Phoenix said, displaying a suspicious grimace. Huxton kept a straight face.

'Driving old equipment and running shorthanded makes them easy targets for bandits. They are bound to have their share of troubles.'

'It's lucky we haven't been the target of any robberies,' said Phoenix furtively.

'Word's gotten around that you work for me,' Huxton explained. 'No one wants you on their back trail.'

'I don't cotton to things like Strap killing the young Yates kid. It's a bad way to handle a situation and bad for public opinion. People around here like the Yates family.'

'The boys are competitive about our rival company. There are bound to be a few arguments or incidents. It's something to be expected.'

'Just so you know, Hux, I won't be a part of intimidating or killing off the competition. I hired my gun for your defense and the defense of the company.'

'That's all I want and expect from you,' Huxton promised.

'Getting back to the new man,' Phoenix went on. 'He wears a gun like most men wear a hat. I'd say he probably has better than average speed. Where did you find him?'

'Alma thought I needed another good hand,' Huxton answered. 'You remember my dear sister-in-law, the one who is financing this little venture.'

'Is she worrying about her investment?'

'Something like that,' Huxton said. 'I mentioned in a letter that the Yates stage had been hit by some bandits. I guess she was afraid we might have trouble getting our wagons through. She somehow learned about Dane looking for work and sent him to us. He demonstrated his speed with a gun for me.' Huxton grinned his satisfaction. 'I'll wager no one is going to take any freight from him.'

'I believe I've seen his name on a Wanted poster.'

'He mentioned having some trouble over in Colorado, but that shouldn't affect his status here in Wyoming.'

'Unless a deputy United States marshal comes through.'

'His past does not concern me,' Huxton said. 'I hired him on as a teamster. He claims never to have lost a load of goods to bad weather, bad luck or bad men. That's as much as I need to know about him.'

'You've got a few unsavory types on your payroll, Hux. That's a fact.'

Huxton did not deny it. 'It's a tough land.'

'So long as you don't expect me to break the law,' Phoenix said. 'I don't intend to end up with my name burned on to a Wanted poster.'

Huxton gave a nonchalant wave of his hand.

'I would never ask you to do anything illegal.'

Phoenix gave his head an affirmative bob.

'I'll be around if you need me.'

Huxton watched the man leave and wondered how a gunman like Phoenix could afford such an inflexible conscience. If it were not for his infernal ethics, he could have used the man to run off the entire Yates bunch.

He let out a sigh. There was nothing he could do about Phoenix. He had other men without scruples. They were not a bright lot, but they followed his orders – whether they broke any laws or not. He would use the willing henchmen to do his bidding and keep Phoenix around for his own protection. The Yates family was near the breaking-point. All it would take was a couple more 'accidents' or robberies.

Huxton felt a tingle of satisfaction. When the time came his offer would not be so generous as the last. He would give them a way out, but they would be left with little more than their lives.

The trip from the mine was along a winding, dust-laden road, one pitted with ruts and rocks jutting from the ground. It was bumpy and rough, but Kyler had some experience of driving a rig. To soften the ride he shifted his weight with each bounce along the road.

The sun sank over the horizon and dusk covered the land. It was about one last mile to the dump-site, where the ore would be loaded on a freight car at the railroad spur. As Kyler rounded a sharp bend a dark figure loomed up alongside the trail. There was a scattergun in his hands!

'Hold fast!' the person ordered in a husky voice.

Kyler pulled on the reins and set a foot on the brake. The team came to a lumbering stop and he stared down the twin barrels of a 12-gauge shotgun.

Veiling his surprise, he greeted the gent with a warm 'Howdy.'

'Climb down!' came the next order.

Instead of obeying, Kyler arched his back to relieve the stiffness in his shoulders.

'Long day,' he said nonchalantly, as if unaware of the shotgun. A fleeting glance at his holster assured him that the thong was not over the hammer of his pistol; the gun was ready for instant use. He put a smile on his face. 'Do you need a ride?'

'I said to get down!' the voice commanded. 'Do it now!'

There was something curious in the bandit's manner of speech, as if the person was trying to make their voice sound much deeper than it was naturally. He judged the size and noticed the riding-boots. This was no ordinary bandit.

'Thanks all the same, but I reckon I'll stay put,' he replied. 'I'm plumb tuckered out from the long haul.'

The twin barrels lifted to aim at his head.

'I said to get down! Or I'll blow you in half with a load of buckshot!'

In spite of the verbal threat, Kyler felt in no immediate danger. The masked person

49

was not going to shoot.

'Beautiful sunset this evening.' He changed the subject, gazing off at the horizon. 'I especially liked the way the sun made the evening clouds look yellow-gold, as if they were on fire.' He returned his attention to the masked individual. 'Reminded me of a gal I met in town. She was something like a firestorm herself, spunky as a colt, yet about as special as if God had taken time to mold her personally.'

The voice wavered and the pitch became much higher.

'Are you crazy?'

'Yep,' Kyler went on wistfully, 'I suspect she's about the prettiest gal I ever laid eyes on.'

The voice was no longer concealed. Jessie's impassioned words exploded.

'Get down off of that wagon or I'm going to shoot! I swear, I'll do it!'

'Miss Yates,' he put aside the masquerade, 'I would admire to do 'most anything you asked, but I'm being paid to haul this freight to the rail head. If there is anything else I can do for you, I'd be proud to lend a hand.'

'You stubborn, contrary moron! I could kill you where you sit!'

The swiftness of his draw was too quick

for a person's eye. With a simple flick of his wrist, he whipped out his gun and aimed the muzzle at the girl.

'And I could have killed you...' his tone grew frigid, 'by mistake!' He frowned down at her. 'Do you know how rotten I would have felt, had I figured you for a real bandit and put a slug between your eyes?' He uttered a sorrowful sigh. 'It would have been an honest mistake, but our kids would have never forgiven me!'

She ignored his silly remark.

'You ... that was incredible.' She did not hide her awe. 'I didn't even see you reach for your gun.'

'Yes, ma'am,' he told her sternly. 'I've never lost a wagon or stagecoach to bandits. I could have pulled iron and shot you at any time.'

'But you didn't.'

'That's because I didn't hire on at this job to kill anyone.'

'How did you know it was me?' she asked.

'I didn't at first, not until I noticed you're wearing the same riding-boots as when we raced our horses in town.'

She looked down at her feet, then heaved a sigh of defeat. Deliberately, she lifted a hand to pull the mask from her face. It was

51

nearly dark, but he thought he could discern a pink hue from Jessie's humiliation.

'Climb on up,' he said, holstering his gun. 'I'll give you a ride to your horse.'

'No, I – I...'

'Where did you leave him? Down at the wash?'

She squirmed beneath his gaze. 'Yes. I thought you would be on the look-out anywhere there was a lot of cover.'

'Well, you were smart about that much,' he told her. 'A driver has to be more cautious wherever there is concealment for a highwayman.'

'I'm not a highway*man*!'

He kept a straight face. 'Climb on up. I'll drop you off.'

'You're a very strange person,' she said, but moved forward a step. She placed the shotgun onto the wagon floor and climbed aboard. Once seated she stared at him with an odd curiosity. 'Who are you?'

He started the team moving before he answered.

'Name is Kyler Dane, and I don't have no fight with you Yates people. I'm a teamster, hired to deliver goods or ore, nothing more.'

'You're working for a crook and murderer.'

52

'So you claim.'

'I don't claim, I know!' She was fervent.

'Got any hard proof?' he asked. 'Anything we can take to the law?'

'What do you mean ... *we?*'

'In spite of your thinking the worst about me, I'm a law-abiding citizen. I don't hold with crooked dealings. At present my job is to drive this team and not let anyone stop me from delivering my load of ore. That's what I aim to do.'

'What about robbing us and turning over our wagons? What about beating our hired hands and stealing supplies from our storage shed? What about pushing my little brother into a fight and killing him?'

'Do you have any evidence that Huxton is involved or ordered his hired men to have those things done, ma'am? Could be you've only had a run of bad luck.'

'You can't be so naïve.'

'Like I said, you need something rock hard to take to the law. If you're only guessing...' He shrugged his shoulders. 'Few men go to prison for another person's suspicions.'

'Huxton has been too smart to make a mistake so far, but he hired the men to ruin us. They are the ones doing his dirty work.'

'Which men are those?'

'Strap Adere, Skinny Davis and Mugs Elder are three of them. I'm pretty sure he also employs the Monger brothers, a couple of real low-life sorts. As for the overall protection of his holdings, he has Phoenix Cline.'

Kyler sobered at the thought.

'I reckon, with a man like Phoenix Cline standing at his side, the odds do favor Huxton.'

'Yes, we don't have a prayer against such a man. Even a United States Marshal would be fearful of taking him on head to head.'

'You're right about that,' he said, pausing to wonder whether Tate had known about Phoenix being involved. Maybe he had chosen Vince for this chore because he thought he might be the one man who would stand a chance against the notorious gunman. If so, he was going to be sorely disappointed. Vince wasn't about to take on Phoenix Cline, not for all the gold in the Dakota hills!

'Stop here,' Jessie spoke up. 'My horse is picketed near here.'

Kyler stopped the team, waited for the girl to climb down and passed her the shotgun. She stood awkwardly, then took a deep breath and heaved a sigh.

'I – I apologize for the impulsive act tonight,' she said quietly. 'It was a stupid thing to do.'

'Yes, ma'am.'

'And I appreciate the fact you didn't kill me.'

'I'm equally glad about that too.'

Then the fire returned to both her eyes and voice.

'But you're on the wrong side of this war, Mr Dane. You should be working for our side.'

'I doubt you could match the wages Huxton is paying me.'

'No, we can't pay a gunman's salary. Since Huxton arrived in Surlock we can't even afford to buy parts for our wagons.'

'So much for the business end of our relationship,' he said. Then with a more earnest tone: 'Concerning other matters of importance, I'd be honored if you would allow me a dance come Saturday night.'

She uttered a groan. 'You really are the strangest man I ever met.'

'Would that be a yes?'

'No,' she said firmly.

'You mean it's a maybe?'

'It's a *no!*'

'I see.' He grinned at her. 'You haven't

55

made up your mind yet.'

'Good night, Mr Dane.' She grated the words. 'The next time I decide to stop you I'll be sure and shoot first!'

'Been a real pleasure visiting with you, ma'am.'

'You keep calling me ma'am and I might still shoot you! The name is Yates!'

'Yes, ma'am.' He showed her a toothy grin, 'I'm right proud to be on a first-name basis with you. Good night, Jessie.'

'It's *Miss Yates!* I didn't give you permission to call me by my first name.'

'And I'm Kyler.' He ignored her correction. Before she could retort with something unladylike he slapped the reins on the rumps of the team and started the wagon moving. 'Goodnight again, Miss Jessie.'

He caught a few of the words she shouted at him, something about him being thick in the skull and born to a family of skunks. He chuckled to himself. The ice was beginning to melt.

Kyler hummed a tune and finished the delivery. It was late by the time he finally arrived back in Surlock. He turned the draft animals into the corral and was thinking of bed when a cocky-looking gent ambled up to him.

'You made pretty good time on your mining runs,' the fellow said.

'And you are?' Kyler asked, noticing the man sported fancy pearl-handled Colts, tied low on either hip.

'Strap Adere,' the man answered. 'I'm a top gun for Huxton.'

'Next to Phoenix, huh?'

Strap shrugged indifferently.

'Some say he's the quickest hand next to God, but I've never seen him in action.'

'I hear he shot and killed the Santa Fe Kid in a stand-up fight. The Kid was supposed to be uncommonly good with a shooting-iron.'

'Never seen him in action either.' Strap dismissed the story. 'If I was sitting on the Yates side of the fence, Phoenix wouldn't scare me.'

'You've been involved in a gunfight or two, have you?'

'I took Cory Yates right on the main street of town some time back,' he bragged. 'Fifteen feet apart when we both drew down – killed him dead before he cleared leather.' Strap uttered a grunt of satisfaction. 'Nope, Phoenix don't scare me none.'

Kyler changed the subject. 'Am I to report in to the boss after each trip?'

'Not unless you had a run-in or some trouble. Me or Mugs will let you know when to make your next haul. You can take a couple days off.'

'Good. I could use a little rest.' Strap swung about and sauntered down the street. He had a swagger like the biggest dog in the pack. Kyler had met his kind a thousand times during his tour with the carnival. All were cut from the same mold: arrogant and cocksure. They thought themselves invincible until someone cut them down to size. He wondered how many lives he had saved by besting and even embarrassing some of those would-be gunmen.

'So, you going to stand out here growing roots like a lame-brain?' Nat asked, having silently come up behind him. 'Or are you ready for a little shut-eye?'

'I'm headed that way.'

'Good enough,' Nat approved. 'You need to get plenty of rest tonight, 'cause I need you to lend a hand with some fencing tomorrow.'

'Fencing?'

'I don't aim to tend horses till one of them kicks the stuffings out of me, sonny boy. I own a little place a mile or so out of town. Got to put up a fence so I can raise me a crop of corn next year.'

'You're going to be a farmer?'

'You got something against farming?'

'Not a thing. I just don't see you wearing bib-overalls and a floppy, worn-out hat, standing out in the sun and hoeing weeds day after day.'

Nat tipped his head in the direction Strap had taken.

'I seen you talkin' to Adere. He likes to think he casts a tall shadow, but Phoenix is the one I'd be watching out for.'

'We all work for the same company,' Kyler replied easily. 'No need for me to worry much about either one.'

Nat snorted. 'I ain't as green as the first blade of spring grass, sonny.'

Kyler frowned. 'What is that supposed to mean?'

'Who do you think sent the letter to Judge Tate? Why do you think I took up all friendly-like with you right off?'

'You wrote the letter?' Kyler asked, surprised. 'But you work for Huxton.'

'The man pays me to tend his animals and have them ready when they're needed. He ain't paying me blood-money to help run the Yates family out of business.'

'You could be at risk telling me,' Kyler warned.

Nat spat a stream of tobacco juice into the dust.

'You're the man Tate sent to handle this chore. I'm curious, how you going to deal with a passel of hostile gunmen?'

'Nothing to deal with yet, Nat. I haven't seen any evidence of wrongdoing by Huxton or his men. I don't think they trust me yet.'

'Yeah, well, whilst you've been walking about with your head in a bucket, I've been doing some proper snooping. There's going to be an "accidental" fire in the next day or two ... out at the Yates place. They have a small ranch west of town where they breed their own draft horses and raise grain and hay for feed. They've been growing and working at this freight business for a good many years.'

'Miss Yates pointed out as much for me,' Kyler told him.

'Anyhow, they've got a big barn, filled with their summer supplies. I overheard Strap and Mugs discussing how to make a fire look like an accident. Them two fellers sure enough intend some mischief.'

Kyler rubbed his chin thoughtfully.

'If I knew when they were going to set the fire,' he said, 'I might be able to thwart their plans.'

'I'll keep an ear to the window and try to find out.'

'I appreciate the help, Nat. This is a big chore for only one man.'

The old man nodded his agreement and spat again.

'Yep,' he gave a snort, 'it's likely a big enough chore to maybe get us both killed.'

CHAPTER FOUR

It was hot the next afternoon. Nat left with a wagon to get a second load of fence posts, while Kyler continued to dig holes. Pausing to wipe the sweat from his brow, he became aware of someone's presence. He pivoted around swiftly, hand dipping toward his gun.

He did not draw, however, as he recognized the visitor as Jessie Yates. She sat atop her big stallion, a few feet from where he had tethered Nipper. The young woman regarded him with an unreadable expression.

'Howdy, Miss Yates,' he said in greeting. 'You're a long way from home.'

'Did you trade in your teamster job to become a farmer?' she taunted him.

'Helping a friend,' he replied.

'There's a surprise,' she teased again. 'You have a friend?'

Kyler put down the shovel and walked toward her.

'I'd admire to be your friend too.' He offered up a genuine sincerity. 'I'm not such a bad guy.'

The young woman tilted her head toward Nipper.

'I thought maybe you'd give me a second chance to beat your nag.'

'Yeah?' he said, looking at her closely enough to detect an odd gleam in Jessie's eye. What was she up to?

'Just you and me this time.' She smiled the challenge. 'If you have the nerve.'

He frowned at the challenge.

'It's pretty hot for running the horses.'

'That's a lame excuse,' she retorted. 'I think you're afraid of being bested by a girl.'

A warning bell sounded in Kyler's head, but he could not figure out her angle.

'What's the wager?'

'If you win,' she replied, displaying an impish simper, 'you claim the prize ... within reason.'

'And if you win?' he asked warily.

'I return with your horse and you walk back – carrying your saddle.'

Kyler paused to consider the contest.

'If I win,' he said carefully, 'you have to allow me a dance next Saturday night.'

Those words caused a frown to cloud her face.

'I don't know about that. My brothers

might decide to string you up with a strong rope.'

Kyler took hold of Nipper's reins.

'I'm not afraid of your brothers.'

'You should be.'

He maintained the dare. 'You're the one asking for a second race.'

She laughed at his bravado.

'Climb aboard your champion, Mr Dane. It's a little over a mile to Miller's Crossing, where the roads intersect. First one there wins.'

'I know the place.'

'Let's go!' she cried. She kicked her horse and took off with a head start.

Kyler swung aboard, ready to pursue the girl.

Nipper snorted from surprise, jumped, then began to buck mightily. Kyler had not yet gotten seated. He held on for about three lunges before he was tossed head-over-heels. He landed on his back and the wind rushed from his lungs.

Through the haze of shock and confusion, he heard a mocking laughter. He gulped in a swallow of air and managed to sit up. When he caught sight of the girl, she was nearly doubled over in the saddle from mirth.

'You should have seen yourself!' she

65

wailed. 'I mean, it was so-o-o funny!'

Kyler took a moment to gather both his breath and his composure. He rose stiffly to his feet and dusted himself off. When he walked over to Nipper, the mare was still wide-eyed and skittish, dancing about nervously.

'Whoa, girl,' he spoke soothingly and patted her on the neck to calm her down. He ran his hand along her back and then lifted up the rear of the saddle, where he discovered and removed a thorny cactus.

'So much for a dance Saturday night!' Jessie jeered in a catty tone of voice. 'Guess you'll have to sit and hold hands with your Huxton pals.'

Kyler began to loosen Nipper's cinch. He wanted to make sure no spines had gotten stuck in her back. He had once known this kind of joke to go askew when an infection from a thorn had caused the eventual death of a horse.

'Where's your sense of humor, Dane?' Jessie ridiculed him.

Kyler masked his displeasure over her prank and managed a flirtatious smile.

'You must be real afraid of letting me hold you in my arms, Jessie. Could it be that you don't trust yourself?'

She flared up at once.

'What are you talking about?'

'You must be worried about keeping a harness on your passions, if you were to get close to me.' He smiled wider. 'But you don't have to worry. I assure you, I'm a gentleman. I wouldn't take an unfair advantage of you during our dance.'

'Why, you pompous, self-loving hypocrite! I'm not attracted to you!'

'Oh, it's OK,' he continued his own teasing. 'I expect you never figured to find a man who measured up against your brothers. It's probably a real surprise, being drawn to me like you are.'

'You ... you...' she sputtered. 'I've never met a man with so much arrogance! I wouldn't dance with you if my life depended on it!'

He smiled. 'We've still got a few days till the shindig. I reckon you'll have time to change your mind.'

Jessie jerked the reins of her horse and spun about. Then she dug her heels into his ribs and took off in a cloud of dust. Kyler allowed himself a smile, watching her race up the gentle slope and disappear over the hill. He had taken a fall, but had managed to turn the tables on Jessie. He felt the maneuver had chipped away another piece of ice.

But is it enough to get her into my arms for a dance? he wondered. If competition was her idea of courtship, she had gained a minor victory at getting him tossed from Nipper's back. He needed to impress her one more time before the dance.

Charles Huxton heard the stage arrive and walked over to the window. It pulled up in front of Yates's express office and the passenger door opened. Huxton groaned as he recognized the first person to step down from the coach. It was Alma Bailey Huxton, the tight-fisted tyrant who had married his brother and financed his freighting operation.

And she had come to town on the Yates's coach!

Huxton quickly donned his freshly cleaned jacket and checked his reflection in the nearby mirror. His hat was perched slightly to one side, not a hair was out of place, and he had taken special care when shaving that morning. He swallowed his dread at facing the woman and hurried out of his office to go meet her.

Alma was on the walk, regarding Big Mike with a critical eye as he unloaded her traveling trunk. She observed Huxton's approach and turned to face him.

'Charles.' She greeted him with a cool reserve. 'I thought I might have to seek you out.'

'I received your message from the telegraph office and have been watching for the stage all morning. Yates is running about two hours late.'

A tight frown furrowed her brow.

'I expected to be riding in our new Concord by this time.'

The word *our* grated on a nerve, but he hid the aversion.

'It hasn't arrived yet.'

Alma backed up so that Mike Yates could not overhear their conversation. 'What about the run to Cheyenne?' she asked Huxton. 'Have you decided how you are going to win the mail and shipping contracts away from our competitor?'

'I've been corresponding with some influential people. Once we have our stage running I'm certain we'll get our share of the business. There's no comparison between a new Concord and that old Troy wagon you came in on.'

'No argument there,' she said crisply. 'I don't think there are even any springs under that wooden bucket.'

Huxton tipped his head in the direction of a nearby eatery.

'They serve a nice cup of tea at the Hot Grub Emporium. I believe they even offer cold lemonade.'

'I'd prefer to get settled in a room first.'

Huxton waved to Skinny Davis. The man hurried over at once.

'Take Mrs Huxton's things to the hotel,' Huxton ordered. Then, looking at Alma: 'I reserved you their best room this morning.'

Alma nodded her approval, but watched after Skinny with an unmasked disapproval.

'Are all of the men working for you of the same caliber as that one?'

'He only does odd jobs.'

'I thought you were serious about this business, Charles. You can't influence people of importance by hiring scruffy, unsavory employees.'

At that moment, Huxton spotted Kyler. He was dressed in a clean suit and had just come out of the barber shop.

'Dane!' he called out. 'Come over here!'

Hearing the name, Kyler stopped and looked around. When he spotted Huxton on the walk he hurried up the street to join him.

Huxton felt an immediate relief as Kyler removed his hat to meet Alma. He had pegged Dane as a gentleman.

'This is one of my drivers, Alma,' he told her. 'Kyler Dane, meet Alma Huxton, my sister-in-law.'

Alma laughed. 'How funny we should finally meet,' she said. 'I'm the one who recommended you to work for Charles!'

Kyler appeared shocked by the news. In fact, he seemed almost struck mute. Charles chuckled. Kyler had obviously thought it had been his brother who had suggested he come to work for Huxton.

'I thought you were a little taller,' Alma remarked to Kyler. 'My husband said you seemed to tower over him.'

Kyler displayed an easy grin.

'And he told me you were merely a handsome gal too,' he complimented her. 'I can see we both made mistakes. He thought I was taller, and you're much prettier than I expected.'

The words of flattery brought forth a complacent smile, but Alma was a businesswoman. She grew serious almost at once.

'What are your thoughts about the situation here, Mr Dane?' she asked. 'I realize you've only been working for Charles for a short while, but do you believe there is a future for this freight line?'

Kyler turned his hat in his hands, as if deciding the correct answer. When he spoke he was blunt and to the point.

'There's a fair amount of work here, but the Yates line has a firm hold in the community. We can compete with them, maybe even undercut them on prices, but they aren't going to give up without a fight.'

'Thank you for the honest opinion, Mr Dane. Good-day.'

'Yes, ma'am,' he said. 'It was nice meeting you.'

Huxton had his jaw anchored to hold back any harsh words. Kyler had told the truth, but that wasn't something he wanted out in the open.

'Seems like a pleasant man,' Alma said once Kyler was out of earshot. 'Not at all like I expected. David said he was on the rough and dirty side, with shifty eyes and a sharp tongue. I found him rather pleasant.'

'Yes, well, you are not a threat to him. I can tell you, he is not a man to rile. I've never seen anyone quicker with a gun than him.'

Alma turned and looked directly at Huxton. She did not waste any more breath on trivial matters. 'I would like to see the company books, Charles.'

'Certainly, Alma.'

'You do remember our agreement?' she asked. 'You asked for six months and your time is up. You must assure me that we will start to make a profit within a few more weeks, or I shall be compelled to withdraw my financial support.'

Huxton lied: 'I'm on the verge of closing some contracts. We are very close.'

'Let's forgo the tea and pleasantries,' she said. 'Send or bring the books over to my room. I'm going to clean up and take a short rest. You can call on me for dinner, let's say about six?'

'Fine,' he replied.

She started to take a step, but stopped.

'Oh, and Charles.' She gave him a sidelong stare. 'I studied accounting principles at Vassar and did much of my father's book-keeping. It would not be wise to try and pass off any altered or contrived figures.'

'I wouldn't think of it,' he said.

'See you at dinner then.'

'Yes, Alma,' he replied, outwardly display-ing an agreeable smile. Inside, a knot of powerless rage formed within his chest cavity.

Kyler walked to the livery before he dared

take a deep breath. Alma Huxton had been the one to OK his being hired! Had she actually met Kyler Dane, his goose would have been in the fire!

He entered the livery barn and discovered Nat busy mending a busted wheel.

'I just met Alma Huxton,' he announced. 'I do believe she's a woman to step aside for.'

Nat gave a bob of his head. 'Gossip has it she is the one who put up the money behind this here freighting venture.'

'That so?'

'Charles's brother married in to her family's money. Alma's pa built a clothing factory back East and made a bundle. He was struck by consumption and headed West for his health, but he died in Denver. Most states don't allow for women to own businesses on their own, so Alma used her money to set other people up and took a cut of their profits. She has financed several businesses in Denver and at least one bank.'

'So she funded her brother-in-law's freight business,' Kyler deduced.

'Yep ... H and B – B standing for Bailey, her maiden name. My guess: she's here to look at the books and see why she isn't getting any richer from her investment.'

'Her visit could prompt more trouble for the Yates family. Huxton is going to be forced to push harder for more business.'

'It's in the works right now,' Nat told him. 'You remember the "accidental" fire I was telling you about?' At Kyler's nod, he continued 'Well, I spotted Strap at the store this morning. He was buying himself a couple five-gallon cans of coal-oil.'

'You think their plan is for tonight?'

'Be my guess.'

Kyler made a quick decision.

'Nipper is probably anxious to get out for a little exercise. Maybe I'll go for a ride this afternoon.'

Nat grinned. 'Best take some fishing-gear with you, in case anyone wonders where you're going. I won't expect you back till morning.'

Kyler's idea was to sneak onto the Yates spread and be in a position to prevent any kind of fire from being set. An alternative plan allowed he might be visiting and inadvertently be at the right place to stop Mugs and Strap. To that end he had done a little reading and was prepared for his next go around with Jessie. If she didn't start shooting at him at first sight, he had a strategy.

Girls were supposed to like poetry and mushy stuff, so he had memorized part of a poem by Tennyson. While he rode, he repeated the words over and over in his head.

Yeah, he had it down pat. The sweet words would surely help to melt another bit of the ice-wall. And, if that scheme didn't pan out, he would try to play the hero by saving the Yates barn. One of the two ideas ought to work in his favor.

Staying away from the main trail, he stuck to the rugged hills and began to follow the creek. The water was not high during the middle of summer. It was twenty to thirty feet across and a couple feet deep, except for pools. There were occasional rocks or a bend in the river's course where calmer waters ran several feet deep.

He was near one such turn when he heard the sweet sound of a feminine voice – a girl was singing ... and splashing! Kyler stopped Nipper in her tracks. Staring through the trees and tangle of foliage, he spotted a saddled horse tied to a bush. The tune was 'Silver Threads Among the Gold', and darned if it didn't sound like Jessie doing the singing!

Kyler did some quick thinking and decided on a bold plan of action. He summoned a deep breath and called:

'Would that be you, Jessie? Or have the heavens allowed an angel to visit on earth?'

There was an audible gasp and a sudden splashing sound.

'Don't you dare come any closer!' Jessie cried out. 'I'm nak...' she hesitated, as if finding naked too *risqué* a word. 'I'm not decent!' she informed him.

'Reckon you don't think I'm decent either,' he replied, nudging Nipper onward. The mare picked her way along the tree-bordered path until they came upon a clearing.

There was a ten-foot high sheer wall of rock carved out of the hillside. The water ran deep and dark beneath an overhanging rim. Within the maze of rocks that protruded above the water's surface, appeared only Jessie's head, her sleek neck and the top of her shoulders.

'How dare you invade my privacy!' she screeched at him.

Kyler stopped Nipper near the edge of the stream.

'Well howdy, ma'am.' He showed her his best smile. 'Fancy meeting you out here in the middle of nowhere.'

'Get out of here!' she snapped. 'I'm taking

a bath!'

'Don't get all riled up, ma'am,' he replied easily. 'I've seen naked hair before – a good many heads and shoulders, too.'

'What are you doing on Yates property?' she demanded to know.

'I came to see you.' With a grin, he added: 'Well, I don't mean *see* you, but you know what I mean.'

'You've got some nerve, invading my privacy!'

He ignored her ire. 'I read something I wanted to share with you.'

'And it won't wait until I'm properly dressed?' she demanded to know, still red-faced at being caught in such a defenseless situation.

'Being that you have no choice, I figure you might sit still and listen.' He excused the intrusion. 'I promise, this won't take but a minute.'

Jessie shivered noticeably.

'Hurry up then. This water is cold.'

Kyler cleared his throat and summoned the words from his memory.

'Let's see, it goes something like this:
There is none like her, none. Nor will be when our summers have deceased.

'Poetry?' She was incredulous. 'You came

to spout poetry at me?'

'You got it, ma'am. I've heard it said that women like that sort of thing.'

'Not while they are freezing, vulnerable and held hostage from their clothing!'

Kyler frowned. 'I don't know that there are any set rules about how a man relates poetry to a girl.'

'Well, finish the silly sonnet and get out of here!'

Kyler returned to the verse. 'Let's see ... *summers have deceased...*' he repeated, trying to remember his place. 'Next comes some gibberish which doesn't make sense for a piece, but I especially like the last part.' He gave her another smile; she continued to glare back at him. 'It goes: *Of her whose gentle will has changed by fate, And made my life a perfumed altar-flame,*' he hesitated. 'Then an odd sort of line about *Eve, from whom she came.*'

Jessie stared at him as if his bacon had slid from his plate in to the fire.

'Is that your idea of poetry?'

'Not mine,' he replied. 'Tennyson.'

'You big dolt!' She gave a shake of her head. 'You can't quote from a master's work and leave out half of the words!'

'You know the poem, do you?'

'I know it has a lot more to it than those few lines.'

He frowned defensively. 'Yeah, but some of the words didn't make sense – *making a sigh for Lebanon*. What's a foreign country got to do with charming a lady?'

'Charming a lady?' She laughed, a derisive and cruel sounding mirth. 'You foolish, two-bit gunman! You haven't got the first idea of how to win a lady's heart.'

'I'm willing to learn,' he countered.

'Ride away, Mr Dane!' she snapped. 'You've ruined my bath.'

He explained. 'I didn't intend to find you here at the stream. I was taking a short cut to your place and heard you singing.'

Her voice rose an octave. 'Go away!'

Jessie was fuming. The red in her cheeks darkened, not from embarrassment, but with her anger. Kyler had failed miserably.

'All I really wanted is for you to allow me a dance with you next Saturday night.'

'Not if you were the last man on earth, Mr Dane. Is that plain enough for you?'

Kyler uttered a deep sigh. 'I apologize for approaching you whilst you were in the water, ma'am. But it was the only way I could get you to let me speak the poetry.'

'Your pitiful reciting of poetry is as

detestable as your working for Huxton. I wouldn't dance with you if it meant saving my life!'

Kyler's self-esteem was squashed, but he summoned a counter attack.

'Miss Yates, I'm for thinking you are the girl of my dreams, but you could sure enough stand to be a little more accommodating. I'm trying to be a gentleman and win your respect proper like, but you won't give me a chance.'

'You're no gentleman! You're a Huxton gunman!' she declared vehemently. 'You're less than human! You're a beast, lower than a wild dog. You deserve nothing but contempt!'

Kyler neck-reined his horse over to where she had piled her clothing on a boulder.

'And you, lady...' he reached down and gathered up the garments, 'could stand to learn a little humility.'

'What do you think you're doing?' she wailed. 'Leave my clothes alone!'

But Kyler ignored her protest. He tucked the bundle under his arm, swung Nipper around and started back the way he'd come. Behind him, from the creek, he heard the echo of Jessie shouting some very unladylike names after him. He knew there would be repercussions for his misdeed, but he was desperate. The dance wasn't that far away.

'Extreme measures for an extremely hardheaded woman,' he said aloud.

He continued to ride until he was out of earshot, then made a wide circle and came in from above the ranch house. He located a secluded cove, picketed his horse and moved to a position where he could keep watch over all of the outbuildings. He had barely settled in when he spied a rider enter the yard. It was Jessie and she had a saddle blanket wrapped around her. She rode up to the front steps of the house, hastily jumped down and dashed into the house.

Kyler smiled to himself. Taking her clothes had been a rotten thing to do, but the gal needed to climb down off her high horse. She could have told him that his attempt at poetry stank without insulting him and calling him names. He had to admit the verse wasn't all that polished, but he wasn't the one who had written it. If Tennyson had used common sense words and made the poetry rhyme, he could have done a lot better.

CHAPTER FIVE

A couple hours after dark, Strap and Mugs arrived. They stopped their horses back in the trees, climbed down and quickly tied off their animals. Each man held a can of coal-oil.

'I'll go around to the back,' Strap said quietly. 'You take the front. Soak everything in sight. When I give you the word, we'll both set fire at the same time and light out for town. The barn will be fully ablaze before anyone can react.'

'Stand where you are!' The order came in a husky whisper. 'If either of you even takes a deep breath, I'll cut you in half!'

Strap and Mugs froze in place and dropped their buckets. Strap lifted his hands. 'Easy, mister,' he said. 'We ain't looking to get killed.'

Five minutes later Mugs and Strap were trussed up with rope and tied, belly-down, over the saddles of their own horses.

'It's downright underhanded to sneak around and set fire to a man's barn,' the husky voice told them. Subsequently the phantom assailant unbuckled their belts and pulled their pants down about their ankles.

'Good thing you're both wearing summer hides,' he said, referring to their drawers. 'Wouldn't want to offend the proper folks in town.'

Strap grunted a muffled oath, but a swat sent the two men's horses trotting in the direction of town. Bound tightly, the two could do nothing but go where the horses took them. The plan to set the Yates's barn on fire had ended in complete failure.

Huxton looked up from his desk as Alma stormed in to his office. His account ledgers were under her arm and a dark expression was on her face. She strode across the room and planted herself in front of his desk.

'Charles, do you have any idea what I saw just now?' she asked.

Her obviously irate tone startled him.

'No, what did you see?'

'Two men, right on the main street of town. They were bound over their horses, with their pants pulled down to their ankles, exposing their … their dungy underwear to the world!' She was livid. 'Adding insult to my mortification, I recognized one of them as the man you had take my things to my room yesterday. He works for you!'

'What!' Huxton leapt to his feet. 'My man was what?'

'An older gentleman from the livery was attempting to free them.'

Huxton doubled his fists and cursed under his breath. Before he could speak, Strap Adere burst in to the room. He skidded to a halt on seeing Alma present.

'Boss,' he said, 'you ain't gonna believe what happened to Skinny and Mugs.'

'Alma has been telling me,' Huxton barked. 'What the devil is going on?'

'They said they got too close to the Yates place. Someone jumped them and sent them to town draped over their horses like a couple corpses.'

Huxton groaned. 'I'll speak to them later. Get them off the street before everyone in town sees them. We'll be the butt of a thousand jokes.'

Strap displayed a stupid grin.

'It's too late, boss ... for being the *butt* of jokes around town, that is.'

'Go!' Huxton snapped.

The smirk disappeared and Strap hurried out of the room. After the man had left, Alma bore into Huxton with a stern look.

'Tell me, Charles, do you purposely hire

men on the basis of their lack of intelligence? Except for the man David and I sent you, the other three I've met constitute two morons and a near-idiot.'

'The teamsters I've hired are good men and no one is going to cross Phoenix Cline. I admit I've got a couple jokers, but I'm holding some high cards too.'

Alma dismissed the discussion and turned to business.

'Do you realize how much this venture has cost me so far?'

'We're about to turn it around,' he defended. 'Once the Concord arrives we'll add the stage-run to our income. Also, I've got an option on a couple more mines.'

'Even if you acquire some new accounts you are going to be in the red for another six months. It will be years before you're able to repay your loan.'

'Once the Yates line fails we'll have more business than we can handle.'

'I'm told their family has been here for years. What makes you so certain they are going to fold and turn over their contracts to you?'

'They have been operating in the red since I arrived and I have arranged it so they can no longer get credit at the bank. They are about finished.'

Alma dropped the account book on his desk.

'My father taught me that a smart business person knows when to cut their losses. I didn't favor the idea of funding one of your schemes, but I wanted to give you a chance to make something of yourself.'

'And it will work!' he argued. 'I only need a little more time.'

Alma put her hands on her hips. Her astringent look nearly crystallized Huxton's blood, but he boldly stood his ground. After a long moment she took a step back.

'I'll give you thirty more days, Charles,' she declared. 'If you are not in a position to start showing a profit by then, this venture is over.' She let the words sink in then asked: 'Fair enough?'

He swallowed his misgivings and gave an affirmative bob of his head.

Alma swirled round and left the room. Huxton held his breath until the door closed. Damn! he thought, able at last to exhale. Alma was one formidable woman. Had she been a man even Phoenix Cline would have stepped aside for her!

'Dave,' he spoke his brother's name, 'if I ever thought of you as being weak or cowardly, I take it back. You have the courage of a grizzly to live with that woman.'

He wasn't called Big Mike because of the size of his nose or mouth. Quite the opposite, Mike Yates was known as a man who minded his own business and seldom offered superfluous words. When he spoke, however, most people listened.

Jessie's brother was standing on the walk as Kyler left his hotel. It took but a glance to know that the man had been waiting for him.

'Howdy ... Big Mike, isn't it?' Kyler greeted him.

'You done rode up on my little sister when she was taking a bath,' the eldest Yates stolidly stated his case. 'I'll be taking exception to that little prank.'

Kyler held up both hands, palms outward, to stop him from continuing on that line.

'It was an accident,' he explained quickly. 'I was taking a shortcut when I happened on your sister. I didn't aim to interrupt her bath.'

'She come home wrapped in her horse blanket,' Mike stated imperturbably.

Kyler swallowed a lump, possibly it was his life's expectancy. 'We exchanged words,' he

88

said, 'and I thought she needed a lesson in manners.'

'My sister's manners are none of your concern.'

'She stayed in the water up to her neck,' Kyler hurried to clarify. 'I didn't see no more of her than her head the whole time we was talking.'

The words bounced off of Mike like so many raindrops striking an oilskin slicker. He began to slip on a pair of work-gloves.

'Had you not been gentlemanly to a point, Dane,' he said, as passive as if they were speaking of the weather, 'I'd have come looking to kill you.'

Kyler uttered a sigh of resignation and dug out his own buckskin gloves. As he slipped them on he tried one last plea.

'I guess there's no talking around this?'

Mike gave a shake of his head.

'What's right is right.'

'OK, but one thing before we start,' Kyler said. 'I would never disgrace your sister. Fact is, I'd admire to come courting.' He nodded to a package tied behind the saddle of his horse. 'I had her clothing cleaned over at the Chinese laundry.'

'Obliged for the courtesy,' Mike said simply. Then he lifted his fists.

With a dread resolve, Kyler raised his guard and prepared for a fight.

The blows came like a hail storm. Big Mike was tough and felt his mission was justified. Kyler used his wits and countered with punches of his own. Five minutes later, both men were bruised and gasping for breath. However, there was no quit in Mike. Once each had gathered their wind, the two of them clashed a second time.

Kyler stood his ground and they exchanged several vicious punches. Neither man went down, but soon the blows began to carry less force. After another five minutes, they both paused folded at the middle, completely winded.

'You wage a good fight, teamster,' Mike eventually spoke.

'I'd admire to ask your sister to dance on Saturday night,' Kyler wheezed between gulps of air.

Mike snorted his contempt.

'Dane, you got more guts than brains, and that's the truth. Jessie has a burning hate for every man jack who works for Huxton.'

'I admit, winning her over is something of a challenge,' Kyler replied.

'You knock me off of my feet,' Mike challenged him, 'and I'll think about giving you permission for a single dance.'

Kyler grunted, still gasping to draw air into his lungs.

'I ain't got the strength to do it,' he admitted. 'My arms feel about as heavy as lead pipes.'

Mike stood up straight. Kyler had the horrible feeling the man had recouped his strength, something he sorely lacked himself.

However, Mike was of a mind to talk, not continue the fight.

'I found a couple cans of coal-oil up the hill from my barn,' he said, staring hard at Kyler. 'I also heard some talk about how Strap and Mugs arrived in town this morning, tied over their saddles, showing off their long handles to anyone with a mind to look. You wouldn't know anything about it?'

'Sounds as if the two of them ran crosswise of some mischief.'

'Where were you headed when you surprised my sister bathing in the stream?'

Kyler shrugged. 'I was on my way out to your ranch to ask if I could accompany Miss Jessie to the dance.'

Mike didn't speak again, but peeled off his gloves. As he walked to the watering-trough Kyler did likewise, shoving his gloves into his back pocket. The spectators who had gathered to watch realized that the fight was over and began to go about their business.

Both men washed the blood from their faces. Kyler had a couple loose teeth and wasn't sure his jaw would still work properly. Still, nothing seemed broken.

'You're pretty handy with your fists,' Mike said eventually.

'I learned how to box from a carnival fighter,' Kyler replied. 'Never fought anyone tougher than you.'

'If you had anything to do with what happened to Strap and Mugs last night you might have to answer to Phoenix. Are you ready to do that?'

'There ain't a man alive ready to take him on.'

Mike cast a sidelong glance at Kyler.

'You're more than you pretend, teamster. I don't know your game yet, but I'll figure it out.'

'Let's just say I'm not your enemy,' Kyler told him seriously. 'I was hired to do a job, but I won't break the law or do harm to you or your outfit.'

'That sounds a bit strange, coming from a man with his name already on a dodger.'

'Mistakes of my youth,' Kyler answered easily. 'I'm not that man any more.'

Mike didn't say another word. He walked over to Nipper, removed the package of Jessie's clothes, then gathered up his own horse. He mounted easily, as if he didn't have a sore or stiff bone in his body. Kyler couldn't say the same for himself. Every muscle in his body ached, he was completely jaded and even his hair hurt.

Jessie did not hide her fury. She dabbed at the cut above Mike's eye so hard that it caused him to flinch.

'Dang, girl! take it easy.'

'Take it easy!' she flared at him. 'You big dumb lummox! I told you, if I hadn't been singing Dane would have ridden right past the pool. You didn't have to do this!'

'He sent you home wearing nothing but a horse blanket.'

'He left me my horse!' she reminded him.

Mike put an inquisitive look on her. 'So why did he take your clothes?'

'Because...' She bit her lower lip and her cheeks darkened with shame. 'I suppose it was partly because I put cactus under his saddle and got him thrown from his horse the other day! I wanted to get even with him for ... for...'

'For winning the horse-race?'

'I let him win!' she snapped. 'I could have cheated and won, but I didn't want to win that way.'

'So that's what this is all about, the race?'

'Not entirely,' she confessed. Mike gave her an impatient look and she offered him a subtle shrug of her shoulders. 'I also tried to take a wagonload of ore away from him the other night.'

'You what?' Mike was stunned. 'You did what?'

'It was a dumb thing to do,' she hurried to clarify. 'I admit it. I took the shotgun and tried to stop his wagon. I was tired of us always being the victim over the past few months. I wanted to get even.'

'You could have been killed!'

She lowered her head again.

'Mr Dane wasn't the least bit intimidated. He took away my gun and gave me a ride to where I'd left my horse.'

'That there fellow is a puzzle.'

'He works for Huxton as a hired gun. That's not much of a puzzle.'

'When I got to town I learned that Strap and Mugs were found at the livery early this morning – tied over their horses, with their pants around their ankles.'

Jessie frowned at the news.

'What do you think happened to them?'

'I'm not sure.'

'You could have asked around,' she said critically, 'if you hadn't been so intent on beating Mr Dane to a pulp.'

'I didn't beat him,' Mike admitted. 'I hit him with my best shots a dozen times, yet he stood his ground. The guy's as tough as rawhide.'

'Being tough isn't far removed from being just plain stubborn and stupid.'

Mike put a curious look on her.

'You're real upset about this.'

'Worthless no-good that he is, you shouldn't have fought with him! He's only been after me because he wanted to...' she didn't finish.

'To what?'

'To dance with me on Saturday night!' She blurted it out.

'He mentioned that to me,' Mike mused, recalling their earlier meeting. 'He told me it was his excuse for being on our land.'

'Yes, that, and to tell me a poem he had tried to memorize.'

Mike laughed at the thought. 'He didn't!'

'It isn't so funny!' She defended the idea. 'It was a verse from Tennyson. It was – would have been – sort of romantic, if he

95

hadn't messed up the words.'

'I didn't know you had been reading Mom's books.'

'A person wouldn't have had to read Tennyson to know the teamster only took bits and pieces out of the composition. He cut words from the middle so the whole thing hardly made any sense.'

'The guy has it bad for you.'

'Yes, and it got him a beating.'

'I didn't break his nose or knock out any teeth,' Mike replied. 'Besides which, he wasn't much to look at before we got after it.'

She finished with the cleaning of the cut and began to wrap his head with a bandage.

'I suppose, as hired killers go, he's not as bad as most of the Huxton men.'

'He told me he wasn't our enemy.'

She tore the strip of cloth at the end and tied it off.

'Keep that on tonight in case it starts to bleed again. I think it'll be OK to take it off in the morning.'

'You don't sound near as upset with Dane as you were yesterday when I seen you scooting across the yard, clad only in a horse blanket.'

She ducked her head.

'It was partly my fault. I shouldn't have been so harsh about his poetry. And he certainly didn't deserve a beating for trying to court me.'

'I never figured you would jump my hide because I defended your honor.'

'I'm only saying I was partly at fault too.'

'Yeah.' He displayed a narrow smirk. 'Sounds more like a lover's quarrel to me.'

'Oh, go to bed!' Jessie threw her hands up into the air and stormed off toward her room. 'Or go hang yourself! I don't much care which!'

Mike laughed to her back, but Jessie did not look round. She was furious at him, at Kyler, at herself – at the whole blasted world!

The man moved like a ghostly shadow, not a walk or stroll but a glide along the walkway. There was an aura about him, a dark foreboding. As Phoenix Cline approached the wagon, Kyler suffered the sinking sensation that he was confronting the Grim Reaper, a bringer of death.

Pausing from checking the team's harness, Kyler looked up to make eye-contact with the deadly gunman. His was an icy gaze, as if he lacked human warmth, while the body merely offered a shell to house his lethal purpose.

'Dane, isn't it?' he asked, coolly appraising Kyler from boot-sole to the top of his weather-worn freighting hat.

'And you'd be Phoenix,' Kyler replied, concealing an inner shudder.

'I hear you're a man with a price on his head.' Phoenix was abrupt.

'Just a misunderstanding at a saloon over Colorado way.'

Phoenix frowned. 'You look familiar. Where else do you hail from?'

'I've been down a few trails,' Kyler evaded.

'I don't recall seeing you before, but I've heard of you.'

'Trouble with a name like Phoenix,' the man replied, 'everyone remembers it.'

'Sounds like something you borrowed from one of those Greek myths.'

'It's an Egyptian myth, actually,' Phoenix corrected Kyler, 'and I've used it for a good many years. It's who I am now.'

'And were you raised from your own ashes?'

'Something like that.'

Kyler allowed the subject to drop.

'So, what's on your mind, Phoenix? Did you come to offer me some tips about how

I could keep my deliveries safe?'

'I'm curious as to where you were night before last.'

'That part of your job,' Kyler evaded, 'to tuck in Huxton's men at night?'

The cold eyes narrowed. Phoenix studied him for any sign of guilt.

'Two of Huxton's boys arrived in town strapped over their horses. They said they were jumped by a gunman over near the Yates ranch boundary.'

'I heard about it.' Kyler showed a grin. 'There have been a few jokes at those boys' expense going around town.'

'You wouldn't know anything else about it?' Phoenix asked.

Kyler arched his brow. 'Nothing more than what I've heard.'

Phoenix regarded his innocent look with a chill scrutiny. Then he let the matter drop.

'I hear you and Big Mike had quite a fight.'

'We didn't see eye to eye over my trying to ask Jessie to the dance.'

His confession caused Phoenix's expression to soften.

'That female is going to be tougher to corral than a Texas tornado.'

'You're not telling me anything new. She

about bit my head off in person, then sends Big Mike to pay me a visit. There's a man I don't want to cross a second time.'

'I'm told you fought him to a draw.'

Kyler laughed. 'I was still on my feet, but that doesn't mean the fight ended even. I'm pretty sure I got the worst of it.'

'The way you wear your gun is familiar.' Phoenix was curious again. 'I saw a man at a carnival once. He had two people stand several feet apart and drop beer-mugs at the same time. He drew and shot both mugs before they hit the ground.'

'Sounds pretty amazing.'

'You wouldn't be him?'

Kyler chuckled. 'If I was that good with a gun, I wouldn't be shagging freight for a living.'

Phoenix studied him again. Kyler had worn a handlebar moustache and a ridiculous outfit when working the carnival. There was little similarity between his carnival character and the man he appeared to be now.

'Yeah.' Phoenix finally grunted the words. 'You wouldn't be him.'

'Why the questions?' Kyler asked. 'Don't those two fellows know who it was who got the drop on them?'

'They never seen his face and didn't recognize the voice.'

'Maybe Big Mike has hired himself a watchdog for his place?'

'Maybe.' Phoenix regarded Kyler with another long look. 'I can usually see it in their eyes,' Phoenix said.

'What's that?' Kyler asked.

'Fear.'

Kyler smiled to hide the tremor of alarm which shot through his body.

'Why should I be afraid of you? We're on the same side.'

'Yes, we are ... for the present,' Phoenix replied. Then he turned about and lifted a hand in farewell. 'I'll be seeing you.'

Kyler watched the man walk away. He moved like a slinking wolf, never looking in any one direction, yet constantly surveying all that was around him.

'What did the honcho want?' Nat asked, having walked up without Kyler hearing his approach.

'He was wondering where I was the night Mugs and Strap came into town tied over the backs of their horses.'

'He buy your innocent act?'

Kyler tossed a quick look at Nat.

'Somewhat.'

'I admire how you risked your neck to stop those two from burning down the Yates place. But if Phoenix finds out, I'll be stomping dirt over your final resting-box.'

'I should think the bruises on my face from Big Mike's beating ought to remove the doubt of anyone else. Most fellows don't beat up the man who saved their barn from being burned to the ground.'

'Unless it has to do with his sister,' Nat pointed out. When Kyler did not reply, Nat continued: 'The boys have always been protective of the only girl in the family.'

Talking about Jessie only made Kyler wish things were different between them. He turned back to business.

'You're the one who sent for help, Nat. How do we prove Huxton is behind trying to run the Yates family out of business?'

'I'm only a hostler, son. You're the smart jack who has to figure that out.'

Kyler thought for a moment. 'Once they trust me, they might ask me to do a job.'

'You're doing the job they want,' Nat replied. 'You make sure no one messes with their deliveries while they raise the devil with every load of freight or stagecoach the Yates bunch tries to move.'

'We can't help the Yates family if we can't

prove anything against Huxton.'

Nat rubbed his chin thoughtfully. 'The local banker threw in with Huxton right off and has cut off any financial help to the Yates family. If he is involved in the overall scheme, he might be the weakest post along the fence.'

'The banker, huh?'

'George Glenn is his name. He's a weasel. Got his stake from marrying a wealthy woman ... who died shortly after H and B Freight came to town.' At Kyler's inquisitive look, he shrugged. 'It might have only been a coincidence.'

'They have a good marriage did they?'

'George's wife dug her spurs into him at every jump seven days a week. He opened the bank, but she was the one who ran the household.' Nat squinted intently. 'She had herself an accident while riding in her buckboard,' he related. 'Her scarf became tangled in the wheel and she was strangled to death.'

'Anyone see it happen?'

Nat grunted his disgust. 'A couple of H and B employees ... Skinny and Mugs.'

'Sounds suspicious. I wonder if there is a way to get to the truth of the matter.'

'You just met Mr Death, sonny,' Nat

alluded to Phoenix. 'You sure you want to test your luck against a man like him?'

'That's the last thing on earth I would want to do, Nat.'

The old gent laughed. 'Yep, it would *be* the last thing you would do too!'

CHAPTER SIX

Kyler had just dropped off his dirty laundry when he came face to face with Jessie.

'I'm glad I found you,' she said, while blocking his path.

'Funny.' He tried to lighten the tension between them. 'I didn't know I was lost.'

No smile. Jessie was obviously concentrating on what she wanted to say.

'I want you to know that I didn't ask Mike to beat you up.' She skewed her face into a frown. 'Not that you didn't deserve a thrashing for taking my clothes.'

'I was going to return them.'

'Yes, Mike brought them home clean and neatly pressed.' Her words were crisp, and she appeared poised like a deer about to spook – one foot in the air, ready to plant it for traction and sprint away.

'That all you wanted to see me about?' he asked.

'Yes,' she was again abrupt, 'What else would I have to say to you?'

'Hum-m,' he said. 'Sure a long way to ride

just to say you're sorry.'

'I didn't say I was sorry,' she countered defensively. 'I merely wanted you to know I didn't ask my brother to pick a fight with you.'

'Why should it matter what I think?'

Jessie threw up her hands. 'It doesn't matter!' she snapped. 'Not one tiny bit!'

He smiled at her flash-fire temper.

'I was about to get some breakfast. I'd be right proud if you'd join me for a bite to eat.'

'I didn't seek you out for a social call.'

Kyler displayed a serious mien.

'You don't have to constantly keep your guard up around me, Jessie,' he said easily. 'My only aim is to court you proper.'

'You're one of Huxton's gunmen!' She spat out the words. 'I could never feel anything but contempt for you! Not in a million years!'

'Only a million?' He grinned. 'At least there's hope for the future.'

'You're an insufferable dolt, Kyler Dane!'

He ignored the insult. 'What would it take to impress you, Miss Yates? There's nothing I wouldn't do for you.'

'You could go take a dive off of the nearest tall cliff!'

He chuckled at her pluck. 'Well, almost

nothing I wouldn't do.'

She gave him another once-over, obviously taking note of the bruises on his face, the swelling around his jaw and the lump over one eye. Mike had dealt him a fair amount of punishment.

'At least this is one contest you didn't win,' she said with a grim satisfaction.

Kyler arched his brows.

'Didn't win?'

'You know, you won the horse-race and you embarrassed me at the creek. You even made a fool of me when I stopped your wagon. It's nice to know you can lose too.'

'You're here, aren't you?' he asked pointedly. At her scowl, he smiled. 'What makes you think I didn't allow Mike to pound on me some, just so you would be forced to come and express your regret?'

'Don't hand me that garbage! You had no choice about taking a beating!'

'And it's right satisfying too.' He ignored her argument. 'It was worth getting a few bruises, just to have you apologize.'

'Apologize!' she screeched. 'I don't know why I thought I had to come into town and humiliate myself. I should have known my brother didn't do you any real harm – he kept hitting you in the head!'

'It don't change the fact you cared enough to make the ride,' Kyler replied. 'I sure do look forward to our having a dance together tomorrow night.'

'Mike will be there, Mr Gunman. You so much as look at me wrong and I'll have him finish what he started!'

'I reckon one dance with you would make another beating worthwhile.'

She jerked the reins of her horse loose from the hitching-rail and swung aboard like a Comanche warrior.

'You're impossible!' she yelled down at him. 'You're the most impossible man I ever met!'

Before he could offer another word, she dug in her heels and dashed away on her horse. She rode out of sight within seconds and Kyler smiled at her hasty retreat.

'By jingo! I do believe I've finally broke through the ice with that there gal.'

Charles Huxton escorted Alma to the coach. He grimaced at the fact Jeff Yates was the man up on the driver's seat.

'I'll be expecting some positive changes, Charles,' she said. Then meaningfully, she added: 'Thirty days.'

'I'll be in touch,' was Huxton's reply.

Alma climbed aboard and shut the stage door.

'I should have waited for your Concord to be in service,' she complained, taking a seat next to the window. 'I'm going to be stiff for a week after riding in this bucket of busted springs.'

'I'm sorry about the delay,' Huxton sympathized.

'Just see to it some of that red ink starts to disappear,' she warned. 'I'm serious about cutting off funding and writing this off as a bad investment.'

'Don't worry, Alma.' Huxton displayed his best smile. 'You'll soon see the returns I promised.'

She didn't speak again. Jeff received the mail sack from the store clerk and placed it under the driver's seat. Then he took up the reins and got the team under way.

Huxton waited at the walk until the stage was well down the street before he was able to take a normal breath.

'Talk about a walking heart attack,' Strap said, having come to stand at his side. 'Your brother must be one tough son to handle her.'

'Yeah,' Huxton grunted, thinking David had probably learned to master a mere two

109

words since his marriage to Alma – *yes, dear!*

'What's the plan, boss?' Strap asked. 'The boys want to get even for that little stunt what got them strapped over the back of their horses.'

'It's a dire situation, Strap, but we'll hold off doing anything until after the dance. I have one card left to play. If it gets trumped, then we'll do this the hard way.'

'Whatever you say, Mr Huxton. You got anything for the new driver? He sure ain't been getting enough work to earn his keep lately.'

'I've been holding him back to drive the new stage. He's the kind of man I want on that run.'

'So we wait,' Strap said.

Huxton gave a nod. 'For the present. If my plan doesn't work out at the dance, we'll open the gate and run the Yates operation out of business.'

'You only have to give the word, boss.'

Huxton didn't speak to him again. He needed to get his best suit cleaned and have his boots polished. He would speak to Jessie. If she refused to see the logic in his offer it would be too bad ... for her and her brothers.

With the town torn between support for the two freighting outfits the dance was a carefully planned affair. In order to mix the single folks and cross the line between each faction the mayor had thought up an idea to promote mingling.

'Gather round, all you single gents!' he called out, bringing a silence to the crowd. 'It's time we raised some money for our new school,' with a smirk, 'and you unattached men can best afford to chip in.'

Almost everyone had shown up for the festivities. Kyler wandered over to where he could see and hear what the game was about. The mayor pointed to the nearby wall.

'If you look here you will see we've got a number of different-colored ribbons spaced along the wall of the barn, one for each of the single girls here tonight.' Then he smiled. 'I'm going to auction off a matching ribbon for each of those on the wall.'

'Why would we want to buy a ribbon?' one man asked.

'The girls are standing outside, behind the side door,' the mayor explained. 'Each of them has a ribbon pinned to her dress. You bid on the ribbon of your choice and you purchase the first and last dance with the girl who holds that ribbon.'

'How do I know who is holding which ribbon?' another fellow enquired.

'You aren't supposed to know which girl belongs to which ribbon,' the mayor answered. 'That's the whole idea.'

There came mumbling and talking between some of the men. The mayor let them discuss it for a moment before raising his hands for silence.

'I don't have to remind you fellows – those who can count, anyway,' he added with a grin. 'But we have only eleven single girls here tonight, between the ages of seventeen and twenty-three. And there are…' he looked out over the group of eligible men and gave a negative shake of his head, 'well, not near enough girls to go round,' he finished. 'That's why we are having this here auction.'

Kyler looked at the row of ribbons. There were a number of plain-colored ribbons and several with mixed colors. The odds of picking the right ribbon to win the first and last dance with Jessie was eleven to one.

'You best have brought some money,' a voice spoke at his side. He discovered Big Mike standing next to him. 'Might take a fair price to buy the last ribbon or two.'

'Could be,' Kyler agreed. 'Must be forty or

fifty single cowboys, teamsters, miners and farmers here tonight, and only eleven girls.'

'I'm glad to see you didn't suffer any lasting effects from our bout.' Mike displayed an odd sort of grin. 'I knew you weren't yellow – except for the bruises that ain't quite healed. Yep,' he shook his head, 'you're kind of a pink and yellow mix.'

'I'd have figured black and blue was more my color.'

'Trust me,' Mike said quietly, a serious set to his eyes, 'you're pink and yellow.'

Kyler did not reply and Mike moved away. The mayor held up the bucket, ready to start the bidding. Kyler wondered why Mike would tell him to bid on the pink and yellow ribbon. Did he have an ally in the Yates family?

'First ribbon is green,' the mayor called out. 'Let's start the bidding at one dollar. That isn't much of a price for the first and last dance with a beautiful girl. Come on, boys! It's for a good cause.'

The bidding began. The green ribbon went for three dollars. The white followed for four. After the blue and orange sold for five each, the bidding became more intense. Four gone and only seven left. Each represented a man's chance to have the first and last dance with a young lady. The red ribbon went for six dollars and Kyler decided it was going to be costly to purchase one of the final ribbons.

'Here's a mixed-color ribbon,' the mayor said, lifting up the next strip. 'It's pink and yellow. How much am I bid for this one?'

'Five dollars!' a man started the bid.

Kyler stayed out until it reached six-fifty. Then he bid seven. Another bid came in higher and he bid eight. After another two bids, Kyler declared:

'I'll bid ten dollars!'

'All right!' the mayor was almost giddy. 'This is more like it! We'll have the new schoolhouse raised in no time!' Then he looked out over the crowd. 'Any more bids on the pink-and-yellow ribbon?' After a moment, he called out, 'Sold! For ten dollars!'

Kyler went forward and exchanged the money for the piece of ribbon. He sure hoped he hadn't paid so much money to dance with Toothless Beda, one of the less attractive girls around town.

The bidding went on for the remainder of the ribbons. The last one sold for eighteen dollars! Kyler felt lucky to have gotten his ribbon before the frantic bidding-war had erupted for the last couple girls.

The mayor displayed the empty bucket. 'The musicians are ready to play,' he called out. 'Each girl will now come forward to stand by her ribbon.'

Kyler held his breath, as the girls came through the side door. One by one, they moved over to stand in front of their own colors. As Jessie took her place, he smiled and experienced a sense of elation. He moved with the other men holding ribbons, walking over to his dance partner.

Jessie blushed and pulled a face at his approach.

'Y-you bought my ribbon?' She was incredulous. 'But how did you...?'

'I believe I have the first dance, Miss Yates,' he answered, handing her the ribbon to prove his claim. 'More important, also the last dance.'

Jessie's complexion darkened. 'Who told you my colors?' she demanded to know. 'I'm going to skin someone alive!' She swept the room with her gaze until she located her brother.

'Hard to be angry with Big Mike,' Kyler said. 'He bought Toothless Beda's ribbon.'

Jessie attempted to hold on to her ire, but her expression gave way to mirth.

'Poor Mike,' she whispered. 'Beda has always had a crush on him.'

'All she needs is a trip to a good dentist, so she can get a set of phoney chompers.'

The music started and Kyler did not waste any time. He led Jessie to the floor and began to dance. It was a slow tune, so they had time to get their rhythm together. As they began to move around the dance area, Mike and Beda came in close.

'I'd better be able to see daylight betwixt the two of you,' Mike warned.

Jessie glared at him. 'Consider yourself lucky to see anything but stars, you traitor!'

Mike pretended innocence. 'What are you talking about?'

She exploded. 'You're the only one who knew my colors!'

He showed a curious smile.

'I figured I was doing you both a favor,' he said.

Before Jessie could respond Mike turned in the opposite direction with Beda and they were quickly out of earshot.

After a few steps and turns, Jessie uttered a sigh.

'I can't believe Mike told you.'

'I reckon he knows true love's blossom when he sees it.'

'It's strictly one-sided. You're still one of Huxton's dirty, leering gunmen.'

Kyler smiled. 'Yeah, but other than that, I'm a right nice fellow.'

'Hah!' she fired back. 'What kind of nice fellow steals a woman's clothes?'

'I left you the saddle blanket.'

'It was rough and coarse and caused an itch for the rest of the day.'

'Winning seems real important to you, Miss Yates,' he explained patiently. 'I had to prove to you I was capable of winning too.'

'By cheating! The same as with buying my ribbon!'

'If I could have afforded it, I would have bought each and every ribbon tonight,' he told her firmly. 'Then I would have let the other ten girls choose their own partner for the first and last dance. You're the only one I wanted.'

'Why? Because you think I'm a challenge? A victory to be won?'

He stared into her eyes, searching, delving deep beyond the outer fringes. They continued to move in rhythm, but the sound of music was lost. Jessie could have lowered her lids to shield her inner feelings and stop the intrusive exploration. However, she allowed the intimacy, until the boldness of

117

the act caused a flush to color her cheeks.

After the lengthy perusal Kyler offered her an agreeable smile.

'I admit you're a challenge, but that isn't why I want to court you. I like what I see in you, Jessie, both inside and out.'

'Like trying to see me at the pool, during my bath?'

'No, ma'am,' he replied at once. 'I sure didn't expect to catch you taking a dip in the creek. That was a complete accident.'

'There are other girls around,' Jessie changed the subject. 'Why not try and court one of them?'

'They don't cause a stir in my gut the way you do.'

'Oh, fine.' She was sarcastic. 'I make you queasy. I guess we do have something in common after all.'

'I reckon mine is a love-sickness,' he said, attempting to counter her remark. 'You maybe need to buy yourself some stomach bitters.'

The first tune ended. Most of the couples parted company. The last dance was promised to the man holding the girl's ribbon, but she was free to dance with whomever she chose until that time.

Jessie stood with Kyler, poised as if still

118

dancing to the music, each of them looking at the other.

'Miss Yates?' A voice broke their timeless stare. 'May I have the next dance?'

Kyler was more than a little surprised to see Huxton standing there. Jessie displayed a curious frown, but she was gracious.

'Of course, Mr Huxton,' she replied.

Kyler felt the light of the world growing dark. Standing there with Jessie in his arms seemed the most natural thing in the world. When she turned to join the interloper he felt his heart slipping away. Nevertheless, he took a step back.

'You don't mind, do you, Dane?'

'The price of being a gentleman is sometimes high,' he replied. Then he looked at Jessie again. 'Thank you for the pleasure of the dance, Miss Yates.'

'You still have claim to the last dance,' she said.

The music started and Huxton spun away with Jessie. Kyler watched, both curious and crestfallen.

Huxton didn't speak until he had guided Jessie to the far side of the barn. When he gazed down at her, Jessie knew he was interested in more than a dance.

'You two seem to getting along rather well for being from rival camps,' he began. 'Maybe it is an inducement for you to trade sides?'

'He happened to buy my ribbon,' she said, dismissing his suggestion. 'I was only allowing him his due.'

'What do you know about him?'

The question puzzled Jessie. 'Why ask me? He works for you.'

'I worry that his devotion to you could compromise the work he does for me.'

She laughed at the idea.

'Other than fight like two dogs with one bone between us, we've hardly said a civil word to each other.'

'Then I can assume your brother hasn't hired the man to be a spy for your camp?'

She continued to scoff. 'Where would we get the money to hire a gunman? We are barely able to stave off the bank! You and your bully-boys, by beating up our drivers, destroying our supplies and looting our wagons, have us nearly broke.'

'I'm a man who gets what he wants, Miss Yates,' Huxton said, not bothering to deny her accusations. 'Perhaps there is a solution for us both.'

'And what would that be?' she asked.

'A bonding union between you and me would bring our two companies together. We could unite the freight and stage runs under one company and both share in the good fortune.'

Jessie was stunned. 'You – are you suggesting marriage?'

'I'm not a bad catch,' he replied easily. 'And I could provide you with a very nice existence. You would be a queen.'

'You and your hired gunmen have pushed us to the brink of financial ruin, but we still have a breath of life left in us and I still have my dignity.'

'I don't want a fight with you and your family, Jessie. I would prefer we join forces and make a company we can run together.'

'And if I refuse?' she challenged. 'I suppose you will have your men force my other brothers into a fight and kill them, the same as Cory!'

'Strap and young Cory's fight was between the two of them. It was not on my orders. I'm opposed to violence.'

'You can't expect me to be so naïve. You've several men working for you who do nothing but rob and harass our drivers.'

Huxton flinched, but continued to guide her about in time to the music.

'My, but you have a low opinion of me.'

'It is well earned,' Jessie retorted.

'You've a feisty nature,' he said with a smirk. 'I do believe a man would have his hands full with you as his wife.'

'It's something you'll never have to worry about.'

He chuckled. 'Take some time to think about my proposal.'

'We're not down to bartering me into slavery yet.'

She was again curt.

Huxton regarded her with a long, hard stare. She felt her body temperature cool under the frosty gaze.

'You might want to seriously think over my proposal, Miss Yates. I'm offering you and your family a chance for survival. A joint venture between your family's company and my own would be an amicable solution.'

She mustered her resolve.

'The answer is no! Mr Huxton. I refuse to be bullied by you and your gunmen.'

The music stopped to end the tune. Huxton bowed shortly.

'Thank you for the dance, Miss Yates. I'm sorry we can't find a peaceful solution to our situation.'

Jessie did not reply, but watched the man

thread his way through the throng of people. He quickly disappeared from sight.

'What did the vulture want?' Mike asked, having come to stand at her side.

'He wants us to join his company in a partnership.'

Mike raised his eyebrows in surprise.

'Do what?'

'Yes,' Jessie said, 'and I'm to be the topping for this cake of a deal. I only have to marry him to make the contract complete.'

'I'm guessing you said no.'

Jessie furrowed her brow.

'Of course I said no!'

'Strange, him offering up an arrangement,' said Mike.

'I'm not exactly the worst catch in the valley,' she objected.

'That isn't my point, Jess,' Mike replied. 'If he is wanting to make a deal with us, he might be at the end of his rope.'

'You think so?'

'Huxton's sister-in-law was in town for a couple of days. We don't know the what or why of her visit, but Jeff overheard her tell him that he had "thirty days" right before she left on the stage. He thought it might only be about getting together again, but it could have had something to do with the fate of his freight business.'

'H and B,' Jessie said, thinking of the name of his company. 'Huxton and Bailey – isn't Bailey her maiden name?'

'Yes. Her family is very well off.'

Jessie felt a glimmer of hope.

'Maybe Huxton is running out of money. Maybe he wants to marry me to save his business.'

'It could be. We just don't know.'

'Miss Yates?' A man stepped forward. 'May I have the next dance?'

Mike gave the man a short once-over and grunted again.

'I don't think you're going to get much rest tonight, Jess. I hope you don't end up with blisters on both feet.'

The music started and she was immediately swept away with the cowboy. Any further discussions with Mike would have to wait until after the dance was over.

Kyler watched from a distance, disheartened, as an entire parade of men sought out a dance with Jessie. What chance did he honestly have with her? She was the toast of the town; she could have her choice of any man in the room.

Nat came over with his third helping of food from the buffet table.

'You ain't et a bite, sonny. That old saying about how a man can live on love only works if his love is for food ... and he's getting all he needs.'

'I might as well eat something,' Kyler acquiesced. 'I won't be able to get close to Jessie until the last dance.'

'Right neighborly of Big Mike to tip you about her ribbon.'

'You noticed who tapped my shoulder for the next dance with Jessie?'

'Huxton,' Nat said, rolling his eyes. 'I never figured him to be romantically inclined toward Jessie. I'd wager he has something else on his mind.'

'Yeah, I wonder what it is?'

'If the man is concerned about you and your loyalty it might be time to pack your things and git. You don't want to tangle with Phoenix.'

Kyler didn't respond, but wandered over and picked up a plate. He would have to wait until the last dance to be with Jessie again. Even as he stood at the refreshment table he saw her laugh at something her dance partner said. The pang of jealousy reared its ugly head, gnawing at his insides. He didn't want her laughing with another man, or smiling at another man, or even sharing the same earth with another man!

Dad-gum, he thought, I've become as insecure as a mouse at a cat picnic!

CHAPTER SEVEN

At last the mayor gave the announcement for the last dance. Kyler approached Jessie and offered up a smile.

'Reckon you're about worn out. I haven't seen you sit down all evening.'

She returned the semblance of a smile.

'The only let-up was when the band took a twenty-minute break. I think I've got blisters on my blisters.'

'We can sit this one out, if you'd like?'

'No,' she answered. 'My brothers would swarm down on us like vultures.'

The music began a slow-tempo song for the final number. Jessie took her position and they started to move.

'I never used to get asked to dance,' she spoke up after a few moments, 'because of my brothers. Most of the boys were afraid to come near me.'

'Yeah, Big Mike's presence is enough to curb most guys' enthusiasm for trying to spark his little sister.'

'Spark!' she said distastefully. 'Not a very

flattering word for romance.'

He chuckled. 'I reckon it's about as romantic as some oaf making gibberish out of Tennyson, huh?'

His humor prompted a laugh.

'You did pretty much demolish the man's poetry.'

'Just goes to show that a man shouldn't try to be something he's not.'

'Oh?' she raised an eyebrow. 'You mean a man shouldn't try to impress a girl?'

Kyler immediately back-pedaled.

'No, I meant he should stick to what he knows. Nothing gets a fellow into more trouble than showing off for a lady.'

'Yes, you're right on that count.'

'I was a little surprised that Huxton asked you to dance,' Kyler changed the topic. 'That's kind of like consorting with the enemy isn't it?'

'It was more personal than business,' she replied.

'You mean he only wanted a dance?'

Jessie's expression hardened and fire leapt into her eyes.

'In case you didn't notice, he wasn't the only one who wanted to dance with me! Brothers or no brothers, I'm not exactly the most undesirable girl in the valley!'

'No, ma'am,' Kyler attempted to extract his foot from his mouth. 'I was–'

'Is it so hard to believe the man finds me attractive?'

'No, ma'am,' Kyler was still reeling. 'I'd be among the first to point out that you sure ain't the lean end of the pork-chop.'

Jessie stopped moving to the music and scowled at him.

'I'm not what?'

Kyler's brain refused to work.

'You know, where women-folk are concerned, you're more the prime cut.' He swallowed his words, abruptly confounded by his poor choice of comparison. 'What I mean is–'

'I know what you mean!' she snapped. 'I'm equal to a piece of meat! A pork-chop! A choice portion of a pig!'

Kyler was in it, right up to his chin. He groped for a way to disarm the beast he had awakened, but he was trapped, without a weapon or a single defense to his name.

'You mangle Tennyson's beautiful poetry!' Jessie scathed him with her attack. 'Then you steal my clothes! You insult and embarrass me at every opportunity and now – now you compare me to a butcher's cut from a hog!'

Kyler released his hold on Jessie and backed up, hands extended, palms outward, to attempt to calm her.

'Miss Yates,' he scrambled to reason with her. 'I didn't–'

'Last dance or not,' she pulled her ribbon from her pocket and threw it into his face, 'I refuse to have anything more to do with an ignorant, uncouth lummox like you! Good night, Mr Dane!'

With those final words, Jessie whirled about and stormed away. Kyler could only watch, helpless, loathing the taste of having both feet firmly entrenched in his mouth. Jeff and Kenny joined up with Jessie, curious at her leaving the dance area in a huff. Kyler knew that even if he had enough wit to conjure up an apology there would be no talking to her at the moment. Her temper was an over-heated forge and it was going to take some time before she cooled down enough for him to approach.

'Dad-gum, Dane!' He cursed his maladroit handling. 'Changing your name sure didn't change the way you mishandle a woman!'

Big Mike stuck with his partner until the music ended. Then he walked over to join his three siblings. He cast a hard look in Kyler's direction, evidently wondering what he had said to insult his little sister.

Kyler didn't stick around. Mortified at his

ineptitude, he left the building and headed for a cold bed and a sleepless night.

Jessie refused to explain her behavior to her brothers until they were on their way home. With Jeff and Kenny in the back of the buckboard, Mike eventually coaxed her into telling them why she had so abruptly parted company with Kyler.

'I was tired,' Jessie admitted. 'I had to be nice to twenty different guys, including Mr Huxton. When Dane came over for the last dance, I wanted to relax.' She sighed. 'I wanted to laugh with him and maybe have him say something nice or flattering.'

'What did he say?' Mike wanted to know. 'If he insulted you, I'll have a few choice words with him.'

Jessie shook her head.

'It wasn't intended as an insult. He just...' her voice grew harsh with her frustration, 'he compared me to a pork chop!'

Mike couldn't help himself. He laughed out loud.

'You're kidding?'

'He asked about Huxton's motive for wanting to dance with me. I said it might have been simple attraction. That's when he decided to compliment me – comparing me to the meaty end of a pork chop ... something like that.'

Jessie didn't realize it, but both Jeff and Kenny had leaned forward to listen. Now they were all in on the conversation.

'What a silver tongue that man has,' Jeff quipped.

'Makes me wish I was a gal,' Kenny also joked. 'It must really feel good to have a guy dote on you enough to compare you to a slab of bacon or a juicy pork roast.'

'Yeah, a prime cut from a fattened hog,' Jeff said back. 'Dang! Kyler Dane is so smooth, he should give lessons on the proper way to woo a lady!'

The boys laughed and Mike joined in. After a moment, Jessie began to laugh too.

'The poor guy,' she said, moved at last by pity for his plight. 'When I started to screech at him, he couldn't back away fast enough. I thought he was going to knock over a dozen people putting distance between us.'

More laughter.

'Have to feel sorry for him in a way,' Mike now took up for Kyler. 'Even when I was trying to beat the stuffing out of him, he asked about courting you.'

'Maybe you hit him one too many times in the head?' Jeff ventured.

'Yeah,' Kenny joined in, 'he maybe don't think so good since you loosened all the rocks in his skull!'

Eventually the ribbing stopped and the two boys sat back in their seat. After a few minutes Jessie turned to Mike.

'There's one other thing Huxton brought up, while we were dancing. He is suspicious of Mr Dane. He even asked if he was working for us.'

Mike grunted. 'I wish he was.'

'Do you think Dane is something more than he pretends?'

Her question caused Mike to ponder on an answer for a time. When he spoke, there was a distinct suspicion in his voice.

'It might only be his affection for you, Jess, but he sure enough strikes me as more than an average teamster.'

'I saw him draw his gun,' Jessie admitted. 'Or, I should say, I saw his gun appear without his hand even moving. I think he might be as quick and deadly as Phoenix.'

'They say Phoenix has no equal.'

Jessie shook her head back and forth. 'I can't believe any human being could be any quicker than Dane ... and he was sitting down at the time.'

'When did you see him pull a gun while

sitting down?'

'When I stopped him on the road,' she said. 'You remember me telling you about it.'

Mike was dumbfounded. 'Yeah, but I didn't know he drew down on you!'

'It wasn't like that,' she said. 'It was a demonstration to show me how dangerous my actions were. He wanted me to know he might have killed me by mistake.'

'Well, he's taking a big chance. If Huxton decides he is helping us, he might send Phoenix to visit him.'

'He didn't give up his wagon to me. Why should Huxton worry?'

'If Huxton learns it was him who stopped Skinny and Mugs from torching our barn, he might decide Dane is on our side.'

Jessie turned on the wagon seat and looked directly at Mike.

'What do you mean – *stopped Skinny and Mugs?*'

'He didn't admit it, but he was the one. I figure he learned those two were going to burn down our barn and came up to our place to stop them. That's when he ran on to you taking your bath at the creek. He prevented the two Huxton thugs from setting the fire, tied them over the backs of their horses and sent them back to town.'

134

Jessie groaned. 'Please tell me you're not serious!'

Mike shrugged. 'Why do you think I told him which was your ribbon?'

'Because you knew about him stopping those men!' she deduced angrily. 'You *knew* and you didn't tell me!'

'I didn't want you feeling indebted to him,' Mike said. 'I've got to think about your reputation. I didn't want the two of you sneaking off to the loft or something.'

'And do what – spark in the moonlight?!' She was furious. 'You should have told me, Mike. All night long, I kept reminding myself that he works for our enemy!'

'He might work for Huxton, but I don't think his loyalty lies with H and B.'

'Why would he risk taking our side in this war, when he is working for Huxton?'

Mike chuckled. 'You really ought to take a closer look in the mirror sometime, dear sister.' A silly grin came on to his face. 'Dane said it himself, you're pretty much the tasty end of the pork-chop.'

'Gads!' she groaned. 'I should have never told you about the pork-chop.'

'Well, you did ask why he would take up against Huxton.'

'I can't believe I'm the only reason for

that.' She rebuked the idea. 'If he helped us, it's because we are in the right.'

'Yeah, sure, I buy that.' Mike oozed sarcasm.

'Darn his hide!' Jessie declared testily. 'Why couldn't he have said something sweet or charming, instead of comparing me to a cut of meat? Now I'm the one in the wrong again!'

'Well, Jess, I wouldn't worry about it.' Mike grinned at her. 'Working for the wrong side hasn't stopped him from chasing after you; my giving him a beating didn't slow him none; and even the threat of going up against Phoenix isn't enough to drive him off. I doubt a few heated words will keep him at bay for long.'

Feeling guilty, Jessie found herself hoping Mike was right. She silently vowed that if Kyler made the slightest effort she would allow him to make up with her. His attempt at flattery had been a total bust, but there could be no doubt he was sincere about courting her. Furthermore, she could not deny that she rather enjoyed the idea.

The next day, the stage was robbed on Jeff's run. There were three passengers and they lost every penny they had, also their watches and jewelry. The following day Kenny left his wagon for long enough to sign some paperwork. When he returned the wagon was gone. He found it in a gully, a mile out of town. The supplies and wagon were both ruined.

The Concord coach had not arrived yet so Kyler returned to hauling ore. After three trips he arrived back at the livery with the team and empty wagon.

Nat helped put up the animals and apprised him of the trouble.

'The war is heating up, sonny,' he finished by warning. 'I'd wager some that the trouble is from Abe and Pete Monger. They've been nothing but trouble since they were weaned.'

'The Mongers, huh?'

'I'm guessing them two are behind some of this here trouble.'

Kyler grunted. 'Probably out of town for most of the stage runs.'

Nat gave a nod of his head. 'And it's been reported that two men, fitting their description, are pulling these stage hold-ups.'

'If we could prove the Mongers are working for Huxton, it would be enough to convict the bull himself.'

'Far as I know,' Nat said, 'the dirty work still comes by order of Strap Adere. There's no direct contact with Huxton.'

'Strap wouldn't make war against the Yates family, unless it was on orders.'

'No,' Nat agreed, 'but you would have to convince a judge and jury of that.'

'Or Strap would have to point a finger at Huxton himself,' Kyler replied. 'We have to do something and soon. If Mike and his brothers decide to fight, it could be a blood-bath.'

'What do you mean, *we* have to do some-thing?' Nat asked. 'I don't recall joining up to fight in this here war.'

'You chose a side when you sent the letter to Judge Tate,' Kyler reminded him.

Nat uttered a whine.

'I knew you was trouble on the hoof, first time I laid eyes on you. I should have listened to myself, but no! I was too blind-stubborn to do it.'

'I need you to keep your ears open. Let me know if and when another attack is coming and I'll take it from there.'

'Oh? That's all?' Nat skewed his face into a sour mask. 'I only have to stick my nose into the snake's den far enough to get it bit off, then you'll take it from there!'

'That's about it,' Kyler replied. 'They still don't trust me enough to talk about any plans when I'm around.'

'All right, I'll put my ear to a few doors and windows and see if I can learn anything of value.'

'Good.'

'What are you going to be doing?'

'I think I'd better talk to Big Mike. The Yateses need to be especially careful right now. They can't get into a fighting war. They have to give me the time I need.'

'Trouble's coming, son,' Nat stated with certainty. 'I see a storm brewing, dark and full of thunder. You sure you don't want to send for some help?'

'Not until I've got proof.'

'OK, it's your grave what's being dug. If your idea don't work out I'll be first in line to kick dirt in your face.'

'Always good to know where I stand.'

'Yeah,' Nat grunted, 'so long as you're able to stand!'

It was mid-afternoon the next day when Kyler rode up to the front door of the Yates house. He stopped Nipper, but did not get a chance to dismount.

'What do you want, Mr Gunman?' a frigid voice asked.

Kyler turned in the saddle far enough to see that Jessie had come from the barn. She had evidently been doing some chores, as she was wearing work clothes and had on a pair of buckskin gloves.

'Good afternoon, Jessie.'

'I warned you about using my first name,' she replied sternly. 'Do you want Mike to give you another lesson in manners?'

Kyler raised both hands in a sign of defeat.

'No, ma'am – Miss Yates,' he rephrased the greeting. 'Matter of fact, Mike is the one I was looking for.'

'He's on the stage run today. Jeff had some trouble with the supply wagon...' She glowered at him. 'He ended up broke down for several hours! He made a thorough check of his wagon before it was loaded, but someone removed the ring pin on the rear hub when his back was turned. The wheel worked itself off and he lost half of his load!'

Kyler lowered his hands and shook his head.

'I don't suppose he saw anyone near his wagon?'

'Huxton and his men are like an icy wind, Mr Dane. You don't have to be able to see it blowing to feel its bite.'

'Remember what I said about proof?'

'We're too busy trying to keep from going broke to dig up any proof. That's why I'm here working at the ranch. Mike thinks it's too dangerous for me to be out driving one of our rigs.'

'I want you to tell Mike not to retaliate against Huxton.'

'So you are finally showing your true colors!' she snapped. 'You've come here to threaten us on Huxton's behalf!'

Kyler sighed. The more he tried to reason with the girl, the more she turned against him. Winning her over was about as hard as trying to swim up a waterfall.

'It isn't a threat, Miss Yates.'

'Just a friendly warning, is that it?'

'You can't win again Huxton. He's got too many guns on his payroll.'

'So where do you stand, Mr Dane?' she wanted to know. 'Did you stop Skinny and Mugs from burning our barn?'

He didn't reply to the question.

'I'm asking you to give me a little time.'

'Time for what?' she demanded to know.

'If I can find evidence linking Huxton to these crimes, we can haul him before a judge and send him to prison.'

Jessie frowned. 'Who are you, Dane? Just what kind of game are you playing?'

'I assure you, it's no game.'

'Are you working for Huxton or not?' she

asked bluntly.

'Yes and no.'

'What does that mean?'

Kyler didn't dare explain any further.

'It means I need for you to trust me. Ask Mike and your brothers to stay shed of any trouble for a few more days. Huxton is ready to turn loose his guns on your family. Don't let them draw you into a fighting war.'

Jessie appeared to think about what he was saying.

'I don't want another of my brothers to be killed like Cory, but we can't take a beating for ever and not fight back.'

'Just give me a few more days.'

'Why should we give you anything?'

'Because I'm on your side,' he told her. 'You have to trust me.'

At last Jessie appeared to relent.

'I'll speak to Mike.'

'I'll be seeing you again,' he promised.

'Yes,' she said wearily, 'I'm sure of it.'

Kyler turned Nipper and headed back the way he had come. As he put the encounter with Jessie behind him, he thought how God must have a great sense of humor.

Bet he spends a lot of time laughing at us poor saps, whilst we are trying to figure out how to please a woman!

CHAPTER EIGHT

Kyler arrived at the livery and heard an angry voice from inside the barn.

'I know you've been snooping around for someone, old man!' It sounded like Strap doing the talking. There came the sound of someone being struck with a fist, then, 'Tell me! Who's in this with you?'

'I told you,' Nat ranted back, 'I was on my way to buy a chaw of tobacca. I didn't hear nothing!'

Kyler tied off Nipper and started toward the barn door,

'I'd wager you spilled your guts about Mugs and Skinny!' Strap sounded furious. 'You told someone they were going to burn down the Yates's supply shed. Who was it, old man? Who did you tell?'

'Go suck on an egg, Adere!' Nat growled back. 'I ain't telling you nothing!'

Kyler moved inside the barn in time to see Strap hit Nat again. This time the old man crumbled on to the floor in an unconscious heap. The gunman drew back a

143

foot to kick him.

'I wouldn't!' Kyler's icy warning stopped him.

Strap looked back over his shoulder at Kyler.

'Yeah, makes all the sense in the world!' he stated. 'It's you and the old wart here. The two of you are in this together!'

Kyler took up a stance, ready for a fight, whether it be with a gun or fists.

Strap turned round slowly to square up to Kyler. 'You're the big man,' he sneered, 'Huxton's tough guy teamster.' He spat on to the straw-strewn floor. 'Well, you don't impress me none, Mr Teamster.'

'You're a pretty tough *hombre* yourself, Strap.' Kyler's tone oozed sarcasm. 'Takes a big man to knock around a guy who's pushing sixty years of age.'

Strap's hand was poised over his gun. 'I aim to show you tough, Dane. You best toss your gun on to the ground and march over to Huxton with me. We'll see how he feels about you working for the Yates bunch.'

'You're the one who better toss away your gun,' Kyler advised. 'You're going to confess that Huxton has put you up to robberies and acts of sabotage against the Yates Freight Company. With luck you won't get

144

more than a couple years in prison.'

Strap scoffed at the idea.

'Huxton was impressed by you being a wanted man and a bad man with a gun, but I ain't seen you draw down on no one. I'm betting it's all talk.'

'You willing to bet your life on that, Strap?'

The man's eyes were aglow. His body tensed, his breathing stopped. Kyler knew the signs all too well. The man was going to draw!

Strap's hand streaked downward and yanked his gun free. His action was smooth and practiced. His thumb caught the hammer of the pistol, as it came out of the holster, cocked, ready for use...

Kyler felt the gun buck in his hand. Strap was fast, too fast for him to take special aim to try and wound him. The round hit him on the left side of his chest and Strap's gun flew from his fist.

In less time than a single blink of an eye, a life was extinguished. Strap sprawled on to his face without so much as a groan. He was dead.

Kyler started to walk over and check on both him and Nat, but a cool voice spoke up from behind him.

'Don't turn around!'

Kyler cocked his head enough to see that Skinny and Mugs had come into the barn. They both had their guns trained on him.

'Looks like Dane has chosen his side,' Mugs said.

'Yeah, and it sure ain't working for Huxton,' Skinny agreed. 'I guess we know who it was who got the drop on us up at the Yates spread. What do we do with him?'

'Strap went for his gun,' Kyler said. 'I didn't have any choice.'

'Drop your iron and step aside,' Skinny ordered.

Kyler did as he was told. While Mugs kept him under his gun, Skinny walked over to Strap. He knelt down and checked his lifeless body. Satisfied he was dead, he picked up Strap's gun and stuck it back into its holster.

'Looks like murder to me,' he said, showing his yellow, tobacco-stained teeth in a sinister grin. 'How did it look to you, Mugs?'

'Never gave him a chance,' Mugs concurred. 'Too bad we arrived too late to stop him from killing Strap in cold blood.'

Skinny chuckled. 'Reckon you're going to hang for murder, Dane.'

Nat was stirring, but he hadn't seen the

fight. Kyler had no one to back up his claim. As he was herded over to a storage shed to be locked up, he wondered how he could prove his innocence.

Kenny arrived at the Yates ranch a few minutes after dark. Jessie, Mike and Jeff were still at the dinner table when he entered the house.

'You ain't going to believe it!' he said, out of breath from his haste. 'That teamster fella, Dane – he killed Strap Adere in a gunfight! There's going to be a hearing in town tomorrow.'

Jessie was struck numb by the news. She felt a darkness cover her world that had nothing to do with the coming of nightfall.

'Kyler killed Strap?' Jeff was equally incredulous. 'What happened?'

'I talked to Nat, but he was pretty fuzzy about the details. He said Strap caught him eavesdropping and dragged him over to the livery to question him. His face had a couple bruises, so I guess Strap was asking questions with his fists.'

'Then what happened?' Jessie wanted to know.

'He was knocked unconscious. When he woke up, Strap was dead on the ground

147

with a bullet through his heart. He said Strap's gun was still in its holster.'

'That's not possible!' Jessie cried, finding her voice. 'Kyler wouldn't kill a man without giving him a chance!'

'Skinny and Mugs claimed to have arrived in time to see the teamster draw down on Strap. They figured Dane was only going to stop Strap from questioning the old hostler. Instead, he up and pulls the trigger and kills Strap right before their eyes.'

'Those two would lie about having a mother,' Mike said tightly. 'I fought with Dane and he didn't hit me with one cheap shot. He isn't the kind to shoot a man down in cold blood.'

'What are we going to do?' Jessie was seriously worried.

'You say the trial is tomorrow?' Mike asked Kenny.

'Going to be one of those hearing-type trials,' his brother replied. 'The retired judge, Buck Taylor, is going to preside over it and determine if there is to be an actual trial. At least he's an honest man.'

'Yes, but he has to find a reason not to believe two of Huxton's men,' Mike said.

'That might be hard to do, considering all four men are supposedly working for Huxton,' Jeff surmised. 'What reason would they have to lie?'

'I told you what Kyler said!' Jessie reminded Mike. 'He came out here to warn us to not fight back for a few days. He was up to something. I'm sure he has been working on a way to help us.'

'I'd say Huxton's men must have figured that out too,' Jeff put in. 'They decided the teamster was working against Huxton and made up a murder charge against him. This here will sure enough take him out of the picture.'

'We can't let him be sent to prison or hanged for taking our side,' Jessie said. 'We have to do something to help!'

All eyes went to Mike, awaiting his decision.

'We'll hold off on any runs tomorrow,' he said. 'Round up every man we have working for us and have them in town for the hearing. We'll try to make sure Kyler gets a chance to tell his side of the story. It's about all we can do for the time being.'

The sturdy blockhouse was used for storing ice, so the walls were thick. Kyler's jailers provided him with a cot to sleep on, a small table with a candle, a pitcher of water and a pan for washing. It was a cell without bars or windows.

Nat arrived about dark with his evening meal. It was not a prisoner's usual plate of beans, but steak and potatoes, with a wedge of currant-pie.

Kyler wasn't hungry, but he ate a fair portion of the meal.

'I'm getting old,' Nat said when he finished eating. 'I can't imagine getting myself knocked out by a punch from a weasel like Strap.'

Kyler shrugged. 'It's not your fault, Nat. I asked you to find out their plans.'

'Yeah, and I got myself caught like some six-year-old kid in a candy store!'

'They haven't proved me guilty yet,' Kyler replied. 'Didn't you say judge Taylor is an honest man.'

'He'll give you a fair shake, but you're playing a game of poker with the deck stacked against you.'

'I might have a card or two up my sleeve to even the table.'

'Oh, I brung you something to pass the time,' Nat said, pulling a book from inside his shirt. 'It's the only reading material you had in your room.'

Kyler had to smile.

'Yeah, I could use a little Tennyson right now.'

'Never figured your sort to read a book about...' he squinted at the title. 'It says: "The Collected Works of the World's Best Poets."' He gave his head a shake. 'Somehow, it don't quite seem like something a man like you would read.'

'Who's on the door?' Kyler asked, turning the subject to something else.

'The Monger boys are taking turns. It wouldn't be a good idea to try anything with either of them. They would be happy to shoot you for having two feet.'

'I appreciate your bringing me a meal, Nat.' He lifted up the book. 'And thanks for this too.'

Nat lowered his voice, careful not to be overheard.

'You want me to send off a telegraph message to Judge Tate?'

'There will be time enough for that if I end up having to go to trial.'

Nat frowned. 'I thought this here was a trial.'

'Only a hearing,' Kyler replied. 'I'm told this judge does things like they do back East. He has a hearing to determine whether a trial is warranted.'

'So he won't sentence you to hang tomorrow morning?'

'No, but he can order a trial as soon as he wants, should he decide to have one. If that comes about, then I might need you to contact Tate.'

'All right, son,' Nat replied. 'You're the one who has his neck on the chopping-block. I'll follow your lead ... until the ax drops. Then I'm picking up my chips and getting out of the game.'

Kyler thanked him for his support and Nat took the empty plate and left.

The single candle didn't put off enough light to do much reading. Besides which, Kyler had too much on his mind to try and decipher the often cryptic messages which were written in poet lingo. He set aside the book, extinguished the candle and lay back on his cot. He doubted he would be able to sleep, but he could close his eyes and hope for a little rest. For his defense he was going to need to be sharp.

Huxton was more than surprised by the visitor, he was shocked down to his socks. There, framed in the doorway, was the most beautiful woman he had ever seen!

'Jessie.' He managed to breathe her name.

'You look stunning.'

Jessie fidgeted nervously. Huxton had never bothered to get a house, only the best room at the hotel. She was embarrassed and uncomfortable, but steadfast in her resolve. 'Won't you come in?'

'No.' She was breathless in her reply. 'It wouldn't be proper.'

He smiled. 'Would you like to go have something to eat or drink?'

'I'm here to discuss the proposal you made, about a joining of our two companies.'

The light of understanding began to over-shadow the dazzling beauty of the girl before him. Huxton was instantly angered at the notion.

'You're here to save that killer's hide!' he growled. 'He's been working for you all along!'

'No, he has not!' she countered at once. 'I don't know what all goes on in Kyler Dane's tiny, sun-parched mind, but it isn't any of our doing.'

'Yet you are ready to volunteer yourself up as a sacrifice to save his hide,' Huxton sneered. 'Why would you do that? If he isn't working for you, why would you offer yourself to save him?'

'You're the one who asked me about a

possible arrangement, remember?' She tried to turn the tables on him. 'You made the overture to me! I only came to discuss the possibilities of working together.'

Huxton hated the idea that Jessie would surrender herself for Kyler Dane. She had flatly refused his offer, but now ... she was willing to barter herself to save Dane!

'That deal is no longer on the table,' he said curtly. 'You had your chance to save your family's company and you dismissed me. Well, now it's your turn. Nothing you can do is going to change Dane's fate. Once Mugs and Skinny tell the judge what they saw, your pal will be held over for a trial. He's going to hang.'

Jessie's hackles bristled.

'Kyler might be smarter than you think, Mr Huxton. You and your lying pals haven't won your case yet.'

'The man hasn't got a prayer.' There was a cruel resonance in his voice. 'Even with you being willing to give yourself up for him, he's as good as dead.'

Jessie didn't reply. She spun about, swirling the skirts of her gown. Then she was gone from sight, striding smartly down the hallway.

Huxton swallowed his passion. It occurred

to him that he might have been too hasty. Perhaps he should have let the girl throw herself at him and beg mercy for Kyler. He could have enjoyed holding her close and kissing those wondrously marvelous lips.

And, when he spurned her, Big Mike would have come to settle for the insult. With Phoenix on the job he would have been rid of Mike Yates. Without him, their freight and stage operation would have been done for.

However, he chose to think he had played it right. Once the Yates company was broke and the entire family was trying to scratch out a living on their pitifully small ranch, he might offer Jessie a second chance to come to him. If she wanted to save her family she could be his bride and he would allow her brothers to work for him. It would be a much better arrangement, and Kyler Dane would not be a part of it in any way!

When the Monger boys opened the door to take Kyler to the hearing, he was awake and sitting in the gloom. He stuck his book into his shirt and went without objection.

The saloon was full of spectators. Kyler spied the Yates clan in the mix, but wasn't able to make eye contact with Jessie. For some reason she appeared subdued, almost ashamed. He wondered about her mood. He had figured she would have been full of fire and ready to either take his side or demand he be burned at the stake!

He had little time for speculation. He was escorted to a chair near the bar, while the judge, Buck Taylor, had been provided with a desk on a small platform. It placed him in a position of authority, where he could look out over the crowd from his chair. The man didn't have a gavel, but used the butt of a gun to hammer on the desk top to call the meeting to order.

'We are gathered for a hearing to determine whether Kyler Dane is to face trial for murder,' he announced in an authoritative voice. 'The prisoner is charged with killing Strap Adere.' He put a hard look on Kyler. 'How do you say, Mr Dane?'

'Not guilty, Your Honor,' Kyler replied.

'We don't have any jack-leg lawyers in Surlock, so I'm allowing you to present your own defense for this here hearing ... unless you have someone else you want to speak up on your behalf.'

'No, Your Honor,' Kyler said. 'I'll talk for myself.'

'As I don't know you, and had very little

156

personal contact with your victim, I will handle the questioning for both the prosecution and defense. Is that acceptable to you?'

'Yes, Your Honor.'

'Very well.' Judge Taylor tapped the butt of the pistol on the countertop. 'I order this hearing to proceed.'

Kyler sat in silence, while both Skinny Davis and Mugs Elder told their story. It was well rehearsed. Each of the men claimed they had walked into the barn at the very moment he had shot Strap down in cold blood. The judge asked for a reason, but neither man could offer a motive, except for the fact that Strap had been getting a little rough with Nat. After their testimony, the judge looked at the livery hostler.

'Mr Osborn, what can you add to this story?'

'Strap liked to walk the big walk,' Nat said. 'He come in and started knocking me around. I didn't see the fight 'twixt him and Kyler Dane, but I can assure you it was a fair fight. Dane ain't no murderer.'

'What was Mr Adere's reason for assaulting you?'

'He and his boys were planning to make some kind of attack on the Yates freight outfit. Reckon you know them boys work for Huxton, and the two express companies are in competition for the freight and stage business hereabouts. Anyway, Strap thought I might have overheard something and was intent on shutting me up.'

'And did you overhear any such plan?'

'No, Your Honor, I got myself caught peeking through a window.'

The judge noted Nat's statement.

'Concerning the actual shooting, you were unconscious for the pertinent part of the fight?'

'By the time I come to, Skinny and Mugs were holding iron on Dane.'

'Thank you, Mr Osborn. That will be all.' Judge Taylor put his regard on Kyler.

'Your turn, Mr Dane,' he said evenly. 'What do you have to say about the shooting?'

'I entered the barn and caught Strap working over Nat Osborn,' Kyler began. 'When I ordered him to stop, Strap turned around to face me. We both had our guns in our holsters at the time. I was willing to settle any dispute with fists, but he went for his gun and I had no choice but to shoot him.'

'What about Skinny's and Mugs's testimony that you killed Strap in cold blood?'

'They didn't enter the barn until Strap was already down. That was when they decided to frame me for murder, by returning Strap's gun to its holster.'

'And why would they want to frame you?'

'They believe I'm the man who stopped them from starting a fire to burn down the Yates's supply shed a few days back.'

The judge frowned. 'Burn down their shed?'

'Yes, sir.'

The judge also filed that information away. 'And were you the one who caught them?'

Kyler sighed. 'Yes, Your Honor. They each had a can of coal-oil, ready to douse the shed and set it afire. I tied them over their horses and sent them back to town.'

'I remember,' the judge said. 'My wife was among those unfortunate ladies on the street who witnessed their unseemly arrival. Why did you do that?'

'It's no secret that I've been trying to court Miss Yates,' Kyler admitted. 'I was going to see her, so I could apologize for an incident which happened between us earlier in the day. That's when I spotted two men sneaking around. It turned out to be Mugs and Skinny.'

'But they work for the same man as you.'

159

'I hired on as a teamster. No one said anything about sabotage.'

The judge frowned. 'I begin to think we might have to look at other charges before this entire affair is cleared up.'

'If I may, Your Honor, I think I can prove to the court that I did not kill Strap in cold blood.'

Judge Taylor displayed curiosity.

'And how would you do that?'

Kyler took a deep breath. 'I would like to perform a little demonstration.'

'A demonstration?' the judge asked. 'One that would clear you of murder?'

'Yes, sir, I believe it would.'

'And what would you need for your demonstration?'

'My gun, two volunteers and two mugs of beer.'

Taylor raised his eyebrows at the bizarre request.

'You want this court to give you a loaded gun and two drinks?'

'Yes, Your Honor,' Kyler replied. 'It's the best way to show the court why I would not have killed Strap in cold blood.'

'I've been a judge for sixteen years, Mr Dane,' Taylor said. 'In all those years, I've never had a request like this.'

'I admit it's out of the ordinary.'

The judge pondered the idea for a moment, but was obviously interested as to what Kyler had in mind.

'Very well, Mr Dane. Let's see your proof.'

Nat brought Kyler his gun. He took it, removed the single spent shell and replaced it with a fresh round. Once it was settled in his holster he looked over the crowd.

'I need two volunteers,' he said.

'I'm one,' Nat said without hesitation.

After a moment's silence, Mike Yates rose to his feet.

'I'm the other one,' he offered. 'What do you need, teamster?'

Kyler had the men step up and gave them each a mug of beer. Then he had them stand facing one another, two steps apart, with a section of the solid saloon wall at their backs. He crossed the room until he was thirty feet away.

'Judge, I'd like for you to count to three, in a smooth, even cadence. Nat, you and Mike hold the mugs out from your bodies, about shoulder-high. At the count of three, let them drop to the floor.'

The judge frowned at the idea.

'You don't intend to draw and shoot both mugs, before they can hit the floor?' He gave a snort of skepticism. 'You trying to get off on a plea of being crazy?'

'If you don't mind, Judge,' Kyler said, beginning to focus all of his concentration on the trick. It had been several months since he had left the carnival. Was he good enough to do this? 'Start the count.'

The judge hesitated for a moment, then began to sound off. His voice was composed, clear and precise.

'One ... two ... three!'

Nat and Mike released their mugs at nearly the same instant. Kyler's muscle memory did not fail him. His motion was swift, smooth and deadly accurate. The sound of two bullets being fired echoed within the room like a single shot. Both mugs shattered from impact before hitting the floor.

There were a number of *ohs* and *ahs* before the room went silent. Kyler holstered his gun and turned to face the judge.

'Strap Adere thought of himself as a fast man with a gun,' he explained. 'He pushed for the fight and, never having seen him in action, I didn't know how quick he was. When he went for his gun, I was forced to kill him ... but it was in self-defense.'

The judge cleared his throat, obviously impressed by the demonstration.

'Uh, having witnessed your display of prowess with a gun,' he began, 'I am inclined to believe you could easily have beaten Strap Adere to the draw. I see no reason why you would have had to murder him. It is the ruling of this court that the shooting was in self-defense. This case is dismissed!'

There were no cheers, but a few people voiced their approval. Strap had done a lot of pushing since he arrived in town. Many of those in the audience had been intimidated by Strap and the other Huxton bullies. He didn't have many friends.

Kyler thanked and shook hands with the judge. He turned around to find Big Mike standing in front of him.

'You aren't going to be working for Huxton any longer,' Mike pointed out. 'How about you throw in with us? We're short a driver or two.'

'I have something to do first,' Kyler replied. 'But keep the offer open for me.'

The crowd had filed out of the saloon, so Kyler and Nat headed for the door. Kyler wished he could figure a way to speak to Jessie, but the opportunity had not presented itself. As he pushed out through the batwing doors the morning sun was in his face. He felt a great relief. He was free. He had been cleared of the shooting without having to disclose his true identity or purpose.

A sudden jolt hit Kyler in the chest like a blow from a sixteen-pound hammer! He heard the vague report of a gunshot, as he staggered into Nat and felt himself falling.

'Someone shot Dane!' a man shouted. 'He's been shot!'

CHAPTER NINE

'I think the bullet came from across the street,' someone said excitedly. 'Anyone see who it was?'

Kyler was aware of people running about, some hollering back and forth, but he was occupied with trying to find his breath, stretched out on his back. Nat hovered over him. A look of grave concern was etched on his weathered face.

'Right through his left shirt-pocket!' Nat exclaimed. 'It don't look good.'

Suddenly, a beautiful, compassionate face appeared. Jessie was there, kneeling down over him. Tears glistened within her eyes.

'Kyler!' she choked out the word. 'Kyler, please don't die!'

Eventually he managed to draw in a breath of air. There was a numbness about his chest but he actually felt very little pain.

'I – I have...' He gulped in a swallow of air. 'There's only one thing I truly regret,' he squeaked out in a hoarse whisper.

'What do you regret?' Jessie asked, leaning

down close.

'That I never got to kiss you,' Kyler replied. 'Hate to die without ever knowing the sweetness of your lips.'

Jessie appeared strangled by her emotion, but she shook her head. 'Don't say that, Kyler,' she murmured. 'You'll be all right. We've sent for the doctor.'

'One kiss,' he repeated. 'It's my last, dying request.'

In spite of the crowd gathered around, Jessie bent down and pressed her lips to his. The pain within Kyler subsided. In fact, he felt nothing but elation over kissing the woman he loved.

'Let me through!' the doctor shouted, pushing past the onlookers.

Jessie rose up at once, but not before the doctor saw what she was doing.

'You starting a new procedure for saving a man's life, Miss Yates?'

'The bullet hit him right there.' She ignored his remark, pointing to the hole in his shirt. 'There doesn't seem to be any blood, but the ambusher hit him square.'

The doctor dropped down to his knees and opened Kyler's shirt. Kyler tipped his head forward, but was unable to see the wound. The doctor paused long enough to reach in beneath his shirt.

'Hummm.' The doctor removed the stout volume Kyler had had inside his shirt and sat back on his heels. 'It would appear you were shot...' he thumbed through the pages and stopped, 'let's see – about two-thirds of the way through the book.'

'What?!' Jessie cried. 'He isn't shot? He's not dying?'

'The bullet is right here,' the doctor said, pulling it from between the pages. 'Easiest surgery I ever performed.'

'Kyler Dane!' Jessie wailed. 'You conniving, under-handed charlatan! You lousy, lying, good-for-nothing sneak!'

Kyler groaned from the effort, but rose up to a sitting position. He lifted a hand to rub the tender spot where the bullet had struck, but he was otherwise uninjured.

'I've never been so humiliated in my entire life!' Jessie steamed. 'You made me kiss you in front of the whole town! You made a complete fool out of me!'

'Nat gave me the book to read while I was locked up,' Kyler explained. 'I stuck it inside my shirt and forgot all about it.'

But Jessie was not to be pacified.

'You can take your stupid poetry and drop dead for all I care!' she screeched. 'That's the last kiss you'll ever get from me!' Then she shoved her way through the throng of people and was quickly lost beyond the crowd.

'You probably shouldn't have pulled that stunt,' Nat said, though he grinned his relief at discovering that Kyler was unharmed.

'It was no stunt,' Kyler argued. 'I thought I'd been hit. You said the bullet went right through my breast pocket. I figured I was dying on the spot.'

'Considering Jessie's reaction, you might have been better off to have been shot.'

'Amen to that,' Kyler said, rising slowly up onto his feet.

'Couldn't find the shooter,' Jeff Yates informed him. 'A few of us took a look around, but whoever it was, he got away.'

'Can't blame him for trying to kill you from a distance,' Phoenix Cline was the one to speak. 'Won't be a man around who wants a piece of you after hearing about your little demonstration in the saloon.'

Kyler drew in a deep breath, still shaky from his close call with death. He hid his apprehension and stared at Phoenix.

'I don't suppose you know who took the shot at me just now?'

'I was behind you as you came out of the saloon, so I didn't see anything. Best guess would be one of Strap Adere's friends.'

'Funny, I didn't think a man like him would have any friends.'

'And I didn't think you were fool enough to buck the long odds, Dane. You go up against Huxton and you go up against me.'

'Even if he's behind robbery and sabotage?'

'I've never heard him give an order to do anything illegal against the Yates line.'

'He'll make a mistake soon enough,' Dane said. 'And I'll be there.'

Phoenix didn't respond to the threat. Instead, he smiled.

'Pretty good trick, shooting those two beer-mugs. I knew I'd seen you before.'

'Glad I could offer you some entertainment.'

'Be seeing you around, Dane,' Phoenix said, flashing him a wink. Then he shouldered a couple men aside and left the gathering.

As Kyler wasn't really hurt, he shook the doctor's hand for coming to his aid.

'Thanks for extracting the bullet from my book, Doc.'

'No charge this go around, Mr Dane,' the doc replied. 'Don't get shot again.'

Kyler nodded at his warning and he and

Nat started toward the livery.

'What now, son?' Nat asked. 'After admitting you waylaid Skinny and Mugs, then killing Adere, you can't figure to be working for Huxton any longer.'

'No, I reckon not.'

'So how are you going to get any proof against the man now?'

'Knowing that Buck Taylor is an honest man, I've got an idea that might work.'

'He's retired from the bench, except for an occasional hearing or local complaint. What help can he be?'

'He can be an honest, reliable witness, Nat. That's all I need.'

Huxton was with Phoenix, discussing the hearing and shooting at the saloon, when Wanda opened the door to his office.

'A town runner delivered this.' She held out a piece of paper. 'He said the telegram was sent as urgent.'

Phoenix was closer, so he took the paper and waited for Wanda to leave. He stared at the piece of paper and uttered a cynical grunt.

'This ought to come as a real surprise, Hux.'

Huxton read the message and swore.

'Kyler Dane is an impostor! The man took Dane's place to infiltrate and destroy my operation.'

'I thought we had ruled out that he was hired by the Yates family.'

'What other answer is there?' Huxton roared. 'He was sent here to ruin me. It's the only thing that makes sense.'

'Hired by who?' Phoenix asked. 'Maybe he's a lawman.'

'If he's a lawman, why not tell the court and have himself declared innocent by reason of doing his sworn duty?'

'Carrying a badge doesn't give a man the right to kill in cold blood.'

'Yes, but it would have probably been enough to convince the judge that he gave Strap a chance to draw against him. You saw our case against him – Mugs and Skinny!' He uttered a snort. 'I wouldn't believe them if they told me the sky was blue.'

'What about these attacks against the Yates line?' Phoenix changed subjects. 'You've been telling me all along that there is nothing illegal going on here.'

'I don't know everything that Strap was up to. He was in charge of keeping our wagons on schedule and overseeing the crew. If he was behind any robberies or sabotage, I didn't know about it.'

Phoenix didn't swallow that answer. 'What would he have to gain by going after the Yates wagons on his own?'

'He hired most of my help. I promised to make him a junior partner once we were making money. He must have gotten it into his head to try and ruin the Yates business.'

Phoenix gave a shake of his head.

'I'm giving notice,' he said quietly. 'I'll stick around for another couple days, because I don't want Dane – or whoever he is – thinking I ran from him. After that, I'll be packing up my things and moving on.'

'You're overreacting, Phoenix. We don't even know what this guy is up to.'

'I intend to check with him before I pull out,' Phoenix promised. 'If he decides to push me you won't have to worry about him at all.'

Huxton watched the man leave the office. Desperation set in. Strap had been the leader of his covert campaign against the Yateses. Without him, he had four mavericks to control. They were all confident about victory, so long as Phoenix Cline was on their side. If he pulled stakes, it would compromise his entire operation. He needed to act fast, before the men discovered that Phoenix was leaving.

'Blast your hide, Dane – or whoever you are!' he cursed the man. 'Why did you have to come to Surlock and ruin everything!'

The plan was a means to end the strife between H and B Freight and the Yates Express company. Kyler had seen and heard enough to know who was doing what, and every act of aggression had come from Huxton's men. It was time to balance the books.

The banker, George Glenn, lived alone in his house except for a cleaning-woman who came by twice a week. Kyler didn't figure Glenn would confess without some pressure, so he devised a little trip for the banker.

It was after dark. Glenn had a habit of smoking a cigar out on the front porch of his house before he went to bed. This night was no different.

Glenn tossed away the nearly spent cigar and rose up from the rocking-chair. That was when Kyler pulled a bandanna up over his nose and slipped up behind him. He put a gun into the man's ribs and hedged his voice with ice.

'Make a sound and I'll bore a hole through you, banker-man.'

Glenn gulped and lifted his hands.

'What do you want?' he cried. 'There's little money in the bank ... no payrolls, hardly any savings either. I'm nearly broke!'

'We're going for a little ride, banker.' Kyler hissed the words. 'You make one mistake and it'll be the last move you ever make.'

'W-what do you want?' Glenn asked a second time.

'Shut up and move!'

Glenn didn't dare look back at Kyler. He went in the direction Kyler shoved him, walking through the darkness until they reached a buckboard.

'In the back,' Kyler directed. 'You make one peep and I'll start shooting.'

Glenn crawled into the bed of the wagon. Kyler covered him with a canvas tarp, then climbed on to the wagon seat and started the team moving. He drove to a secluded spot a mile from town, a place where no one would hear a man scream for help.

Jessie stood at the eating-emporium table, her hands on her hips and glared down at Nat. He took a bite of his supper, but squirmed under the harsh stare.

'I told you, girl,' he whined softly, so as not to draw any attention to their table, 'I don't know where he went off to. The boy don't answer to me.'

'He isn't pretending to work for Huxton any more. Who is he working for?'

'I don't know what you're talking about.'

Jessie leaned across the table, right down in his face. 'Nat! You lying old coot! What are you hiding from me?'

'Look, I don't...' he began, but did one quick chew and swallowed the bite of stew. It went down like a five-pound limestone block. He had to cough and take a quick drink of coffee before he could even manage speech again.

'Huxton knows he isn't Kyler Dane!' Jessie was growing impatient. 'I happen to know he got word today that the real Kyler Dane is in jail! Phoenix is liable to challenge him to a fight the first chance he gets. You have to tell me where he is!'

Nat managed to clear his throat. 'I'm telling you, missy, I don't know where the boy went. He took a buckboard and said he'd be back. That's all I know!'

She glared at him with hot, smoldering eyes, trying to burn a confession out of him. However, Nat did not blink. He had told her the truth. At last, in a show of defeat, Jessie sat down across from Nat.

After a few moments of silence the woman

who ran the café stopped by their table.

'Can I get you anything tonight, honey?' she asked Jessie.

'I don't know,' she answered. 'Maybe a cup of coffee?'

'That's no meal, honey,' the woman said. 'If you don't have the money, I can always use a little help cleaning up.'

'Thank you.' Jessie smiled at the offer of charity, 'but I've got enough for a meal.' After a moment's thought she tipped her head at the plate of food on the table. 'Bring me a plate of stew, same as Mr Osborn here.'

'It's the house special,' said the woman cheerily. 'Four bits and it includes the coffee.'

'Thank you,' Jessie said. 'That should do me just fine.'

As the woman hurried off toward the kitchen to fill her order, Jessie again stared hard at Nat.

'Why a buckboard?' she wanted to know.

'He didn't say,' Nat replied. 'Shucks, gal, the guy has never even told me his real name. You know as much about him as I do.'

'I don't believe that for a minute, Nat.'

The old boy tried to take another bite, but with Jessie's gaze searing into him, he couldn't even open his mouth.

'Dag-nab-it!' he exclaimed. 'If you got to know, I'm the one who sent for him!'

Jessie's mouth was agape.

'You what?'

'That's right,' he said. 'I wrote a letter to a judge I met one time and asked him to send someone to investigate Huxton. He sent Kyler – or whoever he is – to help.'

'But he came in as a criminal?'

'Yeah, he hired on as a teamster, so he could learn what Huxton's men were up to. It also allowed him to see if you Yates folks were playing it straight.'

'And me?'

'What about you?'

Jessie gnashed her teeth.

'You know what I'm talking about, Nat! Why did he try to get close to me?'

'Ye-cats!' he exclaimed. 'This is going to sound like one of them mushy type female stories.'

'Talk!' she snapped.

'He seen you the day of the big July celebration and wanted to know your name. I told him it was no use chasing after you, but the boy is as stubborn as a mule headed for the barn. He never did let his job or duty get in the way of trying to court you.'

Jessie's stew and coffee arrived. She turned over what Nat had told her and took a bite. For some reason, she felt an odd sort of relief, almost a blissfulness. As she began to chew the food she decided it wasn't all that bad.

George Glenn had his hands bound behind his back. He was sitting on the ground, with his legs stuck out so his feet were about thirty inches apart. Two stakes were driven into the ground and a length of rawhide bound either ankle to the stakes, so he couldn't get away. After a few terrified minutes Glenn recovered a measure of composure and put a look of defiance on his face.

'I don't know who you are,' he told Kyler, 'but you can't expect to get away with kidnapping a banker. Come morning, there will be an entire army of people searching for me. You won't get any money. You'll only get yourself hanged!'

Kyler adjusted his mask and tugged down the brim of the hat he'd found. He was wearing a rain-slicker to hide his clothes and build so Glenn had no idea that Kyler was his kidnapper.

'Actually, Mr Glenn,' he disguised his voice, 'I'm not concerned about money.'

'Not robbery?' Puzzlement shown the banker's face. 'Then why have you brought me out here? What is it you want? Who are you?'

'Let's say I'm like a kind of traveling preacher, one who does a little more than spread the word of God. I encourage a man to confess his sins.'

Glenn began to struggle, but he was securely tied. With his wrists and ankles bound he could do nothing but squirm and twist in a sitting position.

'If you let me go, right now, I'll forget about this little escapade. You don't want to end up being hanged for kidnapping.'

'Kidnapping ... murder, it's about the same difference,' Kyler said. 'I believe you know something about *murder*, don't you?'

Glenn's eyes darted about, as if he were searching for an escape route.

'I don't know what you're talking about,' he said.

'Carla ... that was your wife's name, wasn't it?'

Glenn put a long hard stare on Kyler.

'What's my wife got to do with this?'

'Pretty odd coincidence, her dying about the time Huxton's new freight outfit came into town.' Kyler watched for any sign of guilt or weakness. 'Strangled with her own scarf, so the story goes.'

'It was an accident!'

'Yes, well, accidents do happen. One time I saw a poor girl who had gotten her crinoline hoop snagged on the wheel of a buckboard. She would have been dragged to death, if it had not been for some quick thinking person grabbing hold of her team of horses.'

'This was no different,' Glenn stated haughtily, 'Except there was no one around to stop the team.'

'Only Skinny and Mugs, two of Surlock's new arrivals, two of Huxton's men.'

'So what?'

'So, as soon as Huxton started up his express business, you immediately cut off credit to the Yates family. They get hit with a couple mishaps, a lost cargo here or there, and suddenly, they are about to go broke.'

'It was only business,' Glenn maintained. 'I had to keep my bank solvent. With the competition in town, the Yates family was no longer a sound investment.'

'Especially if you knew they were going to suffer some major losses.'

Glenn bulled past the accusation.

'I did what I thought was best for my bank.'

'I think it was all part of the deal!' Kyler's voice was fringed with ice. 'Huxton got rid of your wife for you and you had to return the favor.'

'You're crazy!' Glenn wailed. 'You can't prove that!'

'Maybe not,' Kyler admitted easily. Then he pulled a slender stick of explosives out of his shirt and moved over in front of the banker.

Glenn watched him, fearful, yet curious as to what he was up to. Kyler knelt down and planted the stick in the dirt, between the banker's legs, right up next to his crotch.

'What the...?' Glenn was instantly alarmed.

'Last chance to cleanse your soul from sin, banker-man,' Kyler said, removing a match from his shirt-pocket. 'Your mistress lives in Denver, doesn't she.' It was a statement. 'I'd wager that's where you met up with Huxton. You probably made a deal with him before he came here to start up his freight outfit. He would get rid of your wife and you would cut off credit for the Yates family. He does a service for you and you return the favor by helping ruin his competition.'

'No! No! No!' Glenn blustered. 'You don't know what you're talking about!'

Kyler issued a pronounced sigh.

'Heck of a way to leave this world, with a lie on your lips.'

Glenn fought to maintain his composure. Kyler struck the match to life, touched it to the dynamite fuse and the wick sprang to life, spewing forth thousands of tiny sparks.

'You'll pardon me if I don't stick around,' Kyler said. 'Dynamite makes an unholy mess of a body. I don't want to get blood all over me from being too close.'

'Wait!' Glenn's courage vanished. 'You aren't serious? You aren't going to blow me up!'

'Like an over-inflated balloon,' Kyler assured him. 'I imagine you're going to cover this here area like an oil-painting.'

'But I've done nothing to you!'

'Confession is good for the soul, banker. Maybe you ought to give it a try.'

Glenn yanked against his bonds and tried to scoot away from the burning fuse. Kyler backed away slowly, shaking his head back and forth.

'So long, banker-man. Try selling your tale of innocence to Saint Peter. I'm sure he'll be real sympathetic.'

Glenn broke down.

'No! Wait!' he wailed. 'You're right!' he sobbed. 'I admit it! I was in Denver on a business trip and met Huxton at a casino.' He began to talk fast. 'We were playing cards and got to know each other. We agreed on a plan – he would take care of my wife and I would cut off credit to the Yates outfit.'

Kyler moved to stand over him.

'And the raids on the Yates outfit? You know for a fact that Huxton gave those orders?'

Glenn appeared ready to bawl.

'I heard him order Strap to cause as much damage as possible, in order to break their business.' He stared at the dynamite and rolled his eyes. 'I've told you everything I know! Don't blow me up! Please! Save me!'

'Who all is involved in the robberies and vandalism?'

'The Monger boys were hired to hit the stage once or twice a month, while Skinny and Mugs did the other dirty work. The other men working for Huxton are just teamsters and the like.'

'How about Phoenix Cline?'

'Huxton hired him for his reputation and for protection. Far as I know, he doesn't know anything about the sabotage.'

Kyler bent at the middle and removed the explosive stick. Once he had removed the fuse, he looked back over his shoulder.

'Did you get all that, Judge?'

Buck Taylor appeared from out of the darkness, a look of disgust on his face,

'Carla was my wife's dear friend, George. I can't believe you had her killed.'

'Buck?' Glenn could not hide his shock. He turned his head back and forth. 'No! It wasn't like that!' He whimpered and ducked his head in shame. 'I only said what this crazy coot wanted me to say. I swear! I didn't have anything to do with Carla's death!'

'We'll see what a jury thinks,' Taylor told him firmly. Then he turned about to face Kyler. 'All right, Dane,' he said, 'we have a witness against Huxton. What is your next move?'

'First off, the name is Vince Templeton,' Kyler explained. 'Kyler Dane is a wanted man. Judge Tate sent me here, posing as him, so I could discover what was going on.'

'Templeton,' Taylor repeated. 'All right, son. What do you need?'

'A place to keep our fine banker until I can arrest Huxton and those men who helped in the robberies and destruction of property.'

'There's at least five men against only you,' Taylor said. 'Fast as you are with a gun, I think you'd best get some help.'

'I intend to.'

Taylor gave a bob of his head.

'Deputize anyone you want. I'll stand behind you.'

'Thanks, Judge.'

'As for George here, I've a sturdy tack-shed behind my house. We can lock him up there for the time being.'

'Sounds good,' Kyler agreed. 'I'll get him into the buckboard and we'll haul him back to town. I need to send off a couple wires and then sign on some special help. With luck, I'll be ready to collect Huxton and his boys by first thing in the morning.'

'Get plenty of help,' Taylor warned. 'I don't want a lot of dead bodies.'

'I'm hoping I can take them without a fight.'

The judge grunted his approval.

'I'll second that motion.'

CHAPTER TEN

Jessie searched the town frantically. When she spied Kyler he was standing on the walk, near the corner of the saloon ... confronting Phoenix Cline!

She raced in their direction, fearful of the stern look on the faces of both men. She knew she had only seconds before they both started shooting!

As she drew within hearing distance, she heard Phoenix say to Kyler:

'I always figured you and I would have it out one day.'

Jessie shouted 'No!' and rushed in between the two men. She threw her arms around Kyler, preventing him from drawing his gun.

'I won't let you fight him!' she cried, clinging to him. 'I won't!'

Kyler appeared stunned. 'Jessie, it isn't–'

'I mean it!' she stated adamantly. 'You don't have to prove anything and neither does Phoenix. Even if you are lightning with a gun, he's just as fast. You'll both end up dead!'

Kyler's face skewed into a serious mask.

'Jessie, there are some things a man can't walk away from. A man has to be able to hold up his head.'

'A dead man doesn't hold up anything!' she retorted.

He paused in thought and his tone was contemplative. 'I can think of only two reasons that might keep me from going up against Phoenix with a gun, Jessie.' He stared deeply into her eyes. 'One would be if you were to kiss me.'

She immediately jerked back from him.

'No you don't!' Her anger flared at once. 'I'm not falling for the same line twice!'

Kyler pressed his lips together in a thin line, deadly serious.

'I can't swallow my pride or turn tail and run, not unless it's worth the price. A single kiss from your lips would make a life of shame worth while.'

Jessie hated the mixture of emotions that fought for supremacy within her. She couldn't deny she had enjoyed kissing him and she wanted him to be safe. But she had humiliated herself the previous day. How could she do the same thing a second time?

'It's a small price from you,' Kyler coaxed.

'But it's a high price for me. I have to live

with the decision for the rest of my life.'

Jessie was besieged by the combined heat of passion and a maddening fury at the same time. She didn't wish to give in to his demand, but she couldn't allow the two of them to fight either – not if she could prevent it.

'All right!' she hissed the words vehemently. 'Darn your stubborn, pious nature! I'll kiss you, if you promise not to fight with Phoenix!'

Kyler wet his lips, as if considering the bargain one last time. Eventually he let out a pronounced sigh.

'It's a deal,' he agreed, 'but it has to be a good kiss.'

Jessie rose up on to her toes and placed her mouth against his. She had intended merely to press her lips to his, but once she loosened her passions, the fire burned bright and hot. She kissed Kyler with such zeal that he had to back up a step to retain his balance. Jessie pressed onward, melding her mouth to his in a searing fusion that crushed her lips against her teeth. Her arms hugged him tightly, until she felt her heart pounding only inches from his own. When at last she pulled away they both gasped for breath.

'Hot-dang!' Kyler exclaimed. 'I've never been kissed like that before!'

Jessie lowered her eyes from abashment but murmured: 'I should hope not.'

'OK,' Kyler told her happily, 'I'm a man of my word. I won't go up against Phoenix with a gun.'

Abruptly, a distant alarm sounded within Jessie's mind. She lifted her gaze to put a hard stare on Kyler.

'Wait a minute,' she recalled his words from their earlier exchange. 'What is the second reason you would not fight with Phoenix?'

Kyler appeared to take a deep breath.

'The second reason?'

'You said there were two reasons why you would not fight Phoenix,' she reminded him of his own words.

'Oh, yeah.' He displayed a sheepish grin. 'Well, the second reason is that I would never draw against my own deputy.'

Jessie spun about to face Phoenix. He shrugged and made a brief arching of his brows.

'Jessie,' he said in a matter-of-fact voice, 'meet Vince Templeton, a deputy US marshal. He was just now deputizing me.'

Kyler – now Vince Templeton – displayed an apologetic expression.

'Jessie, honey, I–'

She cut off his sentence with a resounding slap, hard enough to sting her own hand!

'You two-faced, no-good, back-stabbing, double-dealing...' She couldn't think of enough names. 'Blast your sneaky hide! How dare you do this to me – again!'

'Ye-ouch!' he complained, putting a hand up gingerly to finger his smarting cheek. 'Hot-dang, gal! Take it easy!'

'Take it easy!' she fired at him. 'You make me think you're dying and force me to kiss you! Now you've tricked me into kissing you a second time. You know the saying: "Fool me once, shame on you! Fool me twice, shame on me!"?'

'Yeah, but it's sort of your own fault,' he argued.

She was incredulous. 'My fault?'

'If you'd ever let me kiss you, just because I love you, then it wouldn't be necessary to go through all these dramatics.'

'Dramatics?'

'Yeah.' Vince gave an offhand tilt of his head. 'You know, having to go to such wild extremes to get the desired results.'

'You're the most impossible man I ever met!' she cried.

But Vince only smiled. 'I'll say one thing

for you, Jessie, you really are a great kisser when you're angry. I never imagined any gal could kiss thataway.'

Jessie was still flustered but it was terribly difficult to stay angry at a man who continued to flatter and express his devotion with nearly every sentence. As she was trying to decide whether she was more angry or simply frustrated she replayed Vince's words in her mind.

'Wait a minute.' She was struck as she recalled his argument. 'Did you say because I love you?'

'It can't come as any surprise that I'm in love with you,' Vince replied. 'You surely don't think I'd be such an insufferable pest if I only liked you?'

Jessie waved her hand, as if to dismiss the conversation.

'Huxton knows you are not Kyler Dane,' she said to change the subject. 'That's why I came to find you. I wanted to warn you.'

'Yeah, Phoenix already told me.'

'What is your plan now?' she asked.

'I thought I'd ask you to come for a nice romantic walk in the moonlight together,' Vince suggested. 'Then, when everything was quiet and you were a little vulnerable...'

Jessie put her hands on her hips and

scowled at him. 'Vince Templeton, don't make me slap you again,' she threatened. 'Stick to business!'

He raised his hands in surrender.

'Yes, ma'am. Whatever you say.'

'Do you need my brothers and some of our men to help you?' she wanted to know. 'I can have eight or ten men here by morning.'

'I believe Phoenix and I can handle it.'

'Nevertheless, I'll stay at the hotel tonight. If something changes and you two get into trouble I'll be able to go for help.'

'We are going to wait till first thing in the morning,' Vince told her. 'Phoenix said Huxton intends to gather all of his gunmen to outline a final battle plan. We'll have all of the rotten eggs in one basket.'

She looked at Phoenix. He gave her a crooked grin.

'Maybe I ought to ask for a kiss for luck too. I've never been kissed the way you kissed Templeton.'

'If you had you'd be married now,' she told him succinctly.

'No kiss, huh?'

'I'll grant you a smack on the cheek like I gave him afterward,' she offered.

He copied Vince's action by lifting his hands.

'No, ma'am,' he said quickly. 'I apologize for even making the suggestion.'

Vince took hold of her hand.

'I expect to see you, soon as this is over.' He winked, 'We need to discuss our future together.'

'You survive this first,' she retorted, 'then we'll see about anyone's future.'

Vince displayed a comely smile.

'Whatever you say, Jessie.'

'Remember those four little words, Vincent,' she teased. 'You're going to be repeating them for the rest of your life.'

Then she whirled about and left the two men on the porch. She should have still been miffed about being tricked into kissing Vince again, but the deception no longer mattered. He had said he loved her ... and darned if she didn't love him right back!

Vince spent a few hours in bed, but the task which lay ahead allowed him only a few minutes of actual sleep. He was up at dawn and readied himself for the meeting with Huxton and his gunmen. After a quick damp-cloth washing-off he shaved and ran a comb through his hair. Then he spent five minutes oiling and checking the action of his gun. He put in fresh loads, filled his gun belt with ammo and stuck an extra handful into his pocket. He hoped he wouldn't need a single round, but Huxton probably wouldn't go down without some kind of fight.

Phoenix was waiting for him downstairs. He looked well rested, as if he had slept like a baby. The man certainly did not lack confidence.

'Hux called the meeting for seven this morning,' Phoenix said, removing his pocket-watch. 'The boys should be arriving as we speak.'

Vince looked around the room. He had half-way expected Jessie to be there, to give them her support. To cover his disappointment, he said,

'No hotel clerk around this morning?'

'Didn't see him,' Phoenix said. 'He must have slept in today ... or he didn't wish to be here during our war council.'

'You look about as calm as a bear in hibernation, Phoenix. Anyone would think you walked into a gunfight six days a week.'

The man smiled, without mirth.

'You've got that little gal to live for, Templeton. Me, I've got only another job waiting for me somewhere, another selling of my gun.'

'Why not change all that?' Vince asked.

195

'Why not try and find yourself a good woman and settle down?'

'The Phoenix rises from its own ashes, so the myth goes. It says nothing about the bird making a lifelong commitment and settling down.'

'You're not a bird.'

'I had my chance at love,' Phoenix admitted. 'I threw it all away. It was the day I died.'

Vince frowned at his explanation.

'I don't understand.'

Phoenix chuckled. 'Nor do I, my friend. It's a tragic history that I don't wish to rehash in my mind or with another human being.' He lifted his gun and let it settle lightly in its holster. 'You ready?'

'Strap is the only man I ever killed, Phoenix,' Vince admitted. 'I didn't have time to think about it. I hope I don't freeze and let you down.'

'You'll do just fine.' Phoenix was confident. 'If it comes to gun-play I'll take the Monger boys. You take Mugs and Skinny.'

Without another word the two of them left the hotel. Rather than make directly for Huxton's office they turned and went down the walk for a hundred feet. That way, if someone was watching from Huxton's window they would not see them cross the street.

Vince drew on the self-assurance of the man at his side. Phoenix was without fear. He showed no anxiety, no doubt, no hesitation. Vince walked on uncertain legs, a gnawing in his stomach as though he had swallowed shards of glass. His mouth was dry, his palms were moist and his fresh shirt was already damp from nervous perspiration.

Once across the street they moved carefully until they reached the entrance to the express office. Phoenix pushed the door open and looked inside.

'Empty,' he said in a hushed voice, and they both entered the room. They paused a moment to allow their eyes to adjust to the darker interior of the building.

'They'll be in his office,' Phoenix whispered. 'Even if they happened to see us from the window, they wouldn't have known where we were going. Besides which, they don't know we've joined forces.'

Vince put his hand on his gun. The familiar feel helped to calm his nerves.

'Let's get this over with.'

Phoenix led the way, past the desk where the secretary usually sat. The special meeting had been arranged before she was to arrive, so there would be no possibility of witnesses or interruptions. Huxton might trust Wanda with his mail and receipts, but he likely didn't trust her to be around when he declared an open war against the Yates line. They reached the door to Huxton's office and stood to either side. Phoenix looked at Vince and grinned an invitation.

'Ready to play the hero?'

'I just hope I don't let you down.'

'Let me down?' Phoenix said. 'I'm the one working for you – remember?'

'And I'm thanking you now, in case I don't get a chance later.'

'They don't expect us to be together, Vince. We'll take them by complete surprise.'

'Yeah, sounds good.'

Then Phoenix pushed open the door. Vince followed him into the room, ready for anything ... or so he thought.

Jessie was seated in Huxton's chair – bound with rope and a gag in her mouth!

Skinny and Mugs were on their left, Abe and Pete Monger on the right. Charles Huxton stood behind Jessie, a Remington double derringer in his hand, pointed right at Jessie's head!

'Come in, *gentlemen,*' Huxton slurred the words. 'We've been waiting for you.'

Phoenix remained as cool as ice.

198

'I figured you'd want all of us here,' he spoke as if everything was perfectly normal, 'so I brought along Mr Dane.'

'You mean Templeton,' Huxton sneered.

Phoenix grinned. 'He doesn't know we were tipped off about his identity, Hux. I'm thinking he's a lawman.'

'You can drop the act,' Huxton was curt. 'Miss Yates, in an attempt to threaten all of our lives, happened to mention that the two of you had joined forces.'

'I'm a deputy US marshal,' Vince warned him, battling an inner mixture of fear and rage at seeing the woman he loved in danger. 'You and your four henchmen are all under arrest.'

'Maybe you didn't notice, Templeton, but I've got a .41 caliber rim-fire derringer pointed at your girl's head. I believe that gives me the upper hand here.'

Vince whispered to Phoenix, trying not to move his lips.

'What now?'

'The gun isn't cocked,' Phoenix replied softly.

Vince realized he was correct. The derringer pointed at Jessie had to have the hammer pulled back before it would fire. Again, speaking quietly and barely moving his lips:

'I don't have a shot.'

Phoenix smiled to cover his response.

'I'll take him.'

'What are you two whispering about?' Huxton wondered aloud. 'You can't think you can take the five of us? Not with me holding a gun to this woman's head!'

Jessie's eyes were wide with fright, but there was a grim determination on her face. She was ready for whatever happened. Vince flicked a sidelong glance at Phoenix. The man gave a minute nod, showing he was ready.

'The way this is going to happen,' Vince told the men in the room, 'Phoenix and I are going to take all of you into custody. Those of you who choose to fight will die on the spot. We won't try to wound anyone. If any of you draw against us, you'll be killed.'

Huxton laughed at his threat.

'I'm the one holding the gun. Are you blind or just plain stupid?'

'Skinny and Mugs,' Vince ignored Huxton, 'you two are charged with the murder of Mrs Glenn and for vandalism and arson of the Yates wagons and supplies.' He swung his attention to the Monger brothers. 'And you two are under arrest for robbery of the

200

Yates stage ... several different robberies, in fact.' Then he looked over at Huxton. 'Lastly, Charles Huxton, you are under arrest for giving the orders for all crimes committed by these men and Strap Adere, including the murder of Mrs Glenn. I'm also adding the crime of kidnapping.'

He took a breath and surveyed the face of each man, trying to get a read on their probable response. 'Which of you wish to surrender peacefully?' he asked.

The gunmen exchanged looks, but no one spoke up.

'It's settled then,' Vince replied evenly. 'Unbuckle your gun belts or die where you stand!'

Huxton started to laugh, but Phoenix's gun appeared as if by magic. From its muzzle it barked fire and lead hit the man in his gun-side elbow. He howled in shock and pain as the gun flew from his hand. He staggered backward a step, grasping his injured arm.

Vince matched Phoenix's speed, drawing his own gun.

Mugs tried to pull his pistol, but Vince put a round squarely into his chest.

Skinny started to grab for his gun, but immediately stopped in mid-motion. The

Monger brothers were stunned, unable and unwilling to make a move. Staring down the muzzle of Phoenix's gun, they both knew it would have been suicide for them to try and fight.

Huxton's head twisted back and forth, his teeth gnashed in pain and rage.

'Get them!' he cried. 'What are you waiting for?'

Pete Monger pulled a face.

'Me and Abe are only looking at a couple years for them stage robberies. That sure ain't worth dying for.'

Skinny carefully unbuckled his belt and let it drop.

'I can tell the judge whatever he needs to hear,' he said quickly. 'Hux done give the orders. I only done what he told me to.'

The four men were stripped of weapons, then Vince removed the rope from Jessie's hands. She came out of her chair, pulled the gag from her mouth and put a hot glare on Vince.

'What's the idea?' she scathed him with a harsh tone of voice. 'You let Phoenix be the one to shoot Huxton! What kind of a man lets another man save the woman he loves!'

'He had the better angle,' Vince countered. 'I might have hit you!'

'Oh, sure.' She was sarcastic. 'You can hit two beer-mugs from thirty feet away, but you can't stop a man from shooting your fiancée with a peashooter!'

'Phoenix's aim was perfect!' Vince persevered. 'He was on the right side to take the shot. I wasn't!'

'But you couldn't know he was good enough to make the shot!' she continued to argue. 'He has the big reputation, but you didn't know how good he was.'

Before Vince could reply again, Phoenix spoke up.

'I've heard you two kids argue before,' he said. 'I'm going to take these tough guys to jail ... or maybe I should say the judge's tack-shed. I'll see that Huxton is patched up.'

'Thanks, Phoenix,' Vince said.

'Abe and Pete, you two bring along the body of Mugs. That'll keep your hands busy.'

Within a few seconds Vince was alone with Jessie. She was still simmering about the rescue.

'So?' Jessie said, moving over to stand toe-to-toe with him. 'What do you have to say for yourself?'

'I'm glad you weren't hurt,' he said gently,

sincerely. 'If anything had happened to you, I'd have spent the rest of my life tending the flowers on your grave.'

Jessie paused. 'And why would you do that?'

'You know why.'

'Tell me,' she said. 'I want to hear you say it.'

Vince took a deep breath, let it out slowly and looked right into her eyes.

'I might not be a poet, Jessie, but I swear I've loved you since the moment I first set eyes on you. I love you now and I'll love you to my dying day. In all of the world, you're the only thing I want out of life.'

Jessie smiled at him at last.

'Maybe you should have written your own material, instead of trying to quote Tennyson.'

'I didn't want to sound like some sappy kid.'

Jessie slipped her arms around him and looked up into his eyes.

'Sometimes sounding like a sappy kid is OK.'

Vince lowered his head and kissed her gently on the lips. When he rose back up she was smiling at him.

'You have to ask Mike for my hand.'

'Mike knows I'm the right man for you, Jessie. We'll ask for his blessing, but I don't need his permission to love you.'

Jessie giggled. 'I think we can definitely toss out Tennyson. You're going to do just fine on your own, Vince Templeton.' With a subtle wink: 'Yes, you'll do just fine.'

The publishers hope that this book has given you enjoyable reading. Large Print Books are especially designed to be as easy to see and hold as possible. If you wish a complete list of our books please ask at your local library or write directly to:

Dales Large Print Books
Magna House, Long Preston,
Skipton, North Yorkshire.
BD23 4ND

This Large Print Book, for people
who cannot read normal print,
is published under the auspices of

THE ULVERSCROFT FOUNDATION